Ashani Lewis is a novelist and short story writer. She was a winner of the London Writers Awards 2021 in their literary fiction category. She was a recipient of the 2025 Somerset Maugham Award for her debut novel, *Winter Animals*, which was also the winner of the 2025 Betty Trask Prize. Her short story collection, *Everest*, was shortlisted for the 2025 Jhalak Prize. Both books were listed in *Marie Claire*'s 'Best Books Of 2024'.

SUCKER FISH

SUCKER FISH

ASHANI LEWIS

dialogue books

First published in Great Britain in 2026 by Dialogue Books
An imprint of John Murray Group

1

Copyright © Ashani Lewis 2026

The right of Ashani Lewis to be identified as the Author of the Work has been
asserted by her in accordance with the Copyright, Designs and Patents Act 1988.

Quotation on p. 112 taken from Ludmila Ulitskaya, 'Life and Breasts', trans. by Arch
Tait, *Granta*, 131, 23 April 2015.
Quotation on p. 217 taken from Sylvia Plath, 'Lady Lazarus', *Ariel* (London: Faber
and Faber, 1965).

A CIP catalogue record for this title is available from the British Library

Hardback ISBN 978 0 349 70336 7
Trade Paperback ISBN 978 0 349 70337 4
ebook ISBN 978 0 349 70338 1

Typeset in Berling LT by Hewer Text UK Ltd, Edinburgh
Printed and bound in Great Britain by Clays Ltd, Elcograf S.p.A.

John Murray Group policy is to use papers that are natural, renewable and
recyclable products and made from wood grown in sustainable forests. The logging
and manufacturing processes are expected to conform to the environmental
regulations of the country of origin.

Carmelite House
50 Victoria Embankment
London EC4Y 0DZ

www.dialoguebooks.co.uk

John Murray Group, part of Hodder & Stoughton Limited
An Hachette UK company

The authorised representative in the EEA is Hachette Ireland, 8 Castlecourt Centre,
Dublin 15, D15 XTP3, Ireland (email: info@hbgi.ie)

Contents

PART 1: SUICIDES

1.

My mother's running to the river. She tears out of her house, leaving the front door open. She's making a noise that is a sob. The noise catches and breaks and is out of sync with her breath and never stops. She runs to the end of the street and into the road without looking, then down the foothill that takes her into the park, where she trips and falls. She doesn't miss a second; she staggers back up. There are craters in her palms from the gravel now. The park is quiet; the sky is white and threatens rain. Two school kids sit in the bandstand, cross-legged in the unswept leafmould, figuring out how to smoke a cigarette. A parent joggles a pram outside the empty tennis courts. He stares at my mother, streaking across the empty lawns, and lets the pram go still. She's down by the river now, running along the towpath to where it will be deep enough. The park runs parallel to the street where my mother lives, and stretches out along the Thames for miles until the river flows into a lock, at which point the park disperses into a web of disorganised trails and undergrowth. There the water's deep. My mother runs and runs. The sob has lowered, flattened out. Even when it's inaudible, it's still thundering through her. The way her breath is ragged and her jaw hangs open like that. Like an animal's. She can see the lock in the distance. The lock-keeper's cottage is visible on the path ahead, its thatched roof from a fairytale, but all the lights are off and the metal shutter of the little café is down. And she can see, downriver, a weir, three steel sluice gates. The path is less kept here. Thistles, shallow ditches of black mud; loose stones, big as eggs. The trees press in, poplars, bare and spiny. Glimpses of a cycle path through the poplars, better kept but deserted. The water is high, cold, brown with sediment. It moves fast, drawn urgently to the steep, grey spill- ways of the weir. My mother doesn't slow down, but her sob does, pitching high and then flagging, as she lurches to the bank. The surface of the river seems drawn tight. She turns her back to it, then lowers herself in, without pausing. As soon as her legs break the surface, the water takes hold of her sweatpants and she closes her eyes at the sudden weight. The canary grass cuts her hands where she's grabbed for it in fistfuls, but as soon as the water's up to her waist she lets go. The cold is at her ribs. The cold is at her breast. The cold is in her mouth. This is it, she thinks. A flash of neon orange on the cycle path. It doesn't matter. The cold or the current or the depth will get to her before anyone can stop it. My mother cannot swim.

2.

Kolia works as a tutor for a family who live in a gated house on a road of gated houses. She sits at the kitchen table and talks the youngest son through logic questions. The kitchen is big, steel and yellow with his drawings on the walls. The drawings are regulation-grade kid scribbles but they look good in the kitchen; they've been framed professionally. The frames are massive but thin, skinny strips of polished wood, with most of the space inside taken up by the paper mount. The mounts, which are about a metre squared of white card, have these tiny apertures, about ten by ten, showing off a picture the size of a postcard. The effect is very expensive, Kolia thinks. It turns totally mediocre child-drawings into real art: the expansive, cream-coloured surroundings lend a gravity to the scrawled dragon or waxy rainbow, which, tacked onto a fridge, might be immediately dismissed.

The boy's chief nanny stands behind the glint of the kitchen island. Kolia doesn't think she's ever seen Devna sit down. It wouldn't surprise her if Devna isn't allowed to sit down. Every day that Kolia comes over to teach, Devna is standing behind the kitchen island, scooping seeds out of pomegranates, pomegranate after pomegranate. The family's fridge is filled with expensive glass Tupperware, and the Tupperware is filled with pomegranate seeds. Kolia used to teach English to their older son but he's now at boarding school, so it's just her and Enzo, and logic. The logic questions are to prepare Enzo for an entrance exam that he'll take when he's eight, because his mother is certain that eight is when Enzo will be at his very cleverest.

There are various elements to the work that make Kolia slightly uncomfortable. She's conscious of Devna's frosty stare over the pomegranates, and suspects that she's aware of the difference in their hourly pay. But so many of Kolia's friends work as private tutors. The hours are flexible and the pay is madly disproportionate to the work. It's funny, a host of grafters in their early twenties, not quite ready for a nine-to-five, living off salaries that mean nothing to parents of St Paul's or City or Charterhouse Nursery. Like the suckerfish that live inside the shark, brushing its big teeth.

('It's one of those things,' Mia had said. 'You have to spin it. Like: I'm exploiting *them*, Mum.' Kolia hasn't spoken to her mother in months, but Mia is a great suckerfish and her best friend, so she'd just nodded. She'd met Mia's student once. He was in the same year as Enzo, and Kolia had supervised their playdate. She'd heard terrible things about Theo, whose parents had asked Mia to stay with them at their summer home so that he could get ahead on work over the holidays. Theo had made up his own summer job, a Get-Rich-Quick scheme in the style of Horrid Henry or the Bastables. He was going to get a peacock and sell its feathers individually to all the other tasteful seven-year-olds. He'd taken the idea hilariously seriously, drawing up plans and estimating profit, and Mia thought it was funny; she said that she could see the dollar signs in his eyes. But then she'd found him after a lesson one day, crying hotly over the dull body of a real Indian peacock. He was too upset to go through with the selling. Mia told the story with more sympathy than horror. 'You know when you're a kid,' she'd said to Kolia, 'and you have a really good idea, the best idea ever, and it's going to make you rich or famous or happy . . . You're going to draw a crocodile that's so scary that everyone thinks you have a real crocodile. Or you're going to sell friendship bracelets until you have enough money to buy a house. And then you get to work and halfway through, you realise it's just shit. Like it's a shit, crayoned drawing of a crocodile. Or, it's an ugly scoubidou bracelet that doesn't actually go all the way around anyone's hand. It was like that, times a million.'

Theo had seemed fine when Kolia had met him. His mother had picked him up early, a blonde with expensive make-up that had run in the heat. She hadn't looked bad: she'd looked melty, but tan and poreless. 'Thanks, Devna,' she'd said to Kolia; 'Bye, Enzo.')

Enzo's mother, Francesca, doesn't work. She does her make-up in long slashes; she looks like she's stepped out of a Futurist painting, with her wardrobe full of Fascist lines – sharp collars, straight hems, perfect white right angles for cuffs. She's not a lovely, floury Italian; neither is Enzo, though he has the features of an angel. No, Enzo's more like a sinister giallo marionette. The family have a chief nanny and a secondary nanny and a cook and a cleaner, all of whom are women, all of whom have known Enzo since he was born. They mostly seem to adore him. He shouts at them and cries at them and makes them smell his fingers – once Kolia saw him sink his teeth into Devna's leg like an animal. Enzo's imaginary friend is a little boy whose head has fallen off.

God, all the steel and yellow's starting to get on Kolia's nerves. The logic question trembles on the paper in front of her.

Assume that some pings are lings, all hings are fings, and some tings are pings.
Therefore it makes sense that:

A: some lings may also be tings
B: all pings are lings
C: all hings are tings
D: some fings are lings
E: all hings are pings

Why would anyone want a school full of children who've been trained to think in this way? Kolia stares at the words until they blur, and then says 'Okay, so, we're going to have a look at a different question style now.' She turns the page with authority.

'What about question seven?' says Enzo, infuriatingly. She hopes Devna didn't hear.

'No, Enzo, I want you to have a go at number eight. It's a format we haven't seen yet, and it's all over the past papers.'

Three of the following words are alike in some way. Which is the odd word out?
A: needle
B: thread
C: wool
D: knit

This question is accompanied by a black-and-white stock photo of a woman knitting. The question paper has been photocopied from a book of practice tests, and the photograph has that distinctive photocopied effect. The edges are soft, the ball of wool is overexposed so that the strands of yarn bleed together, black and white. Kolia had once been to an exhibition of Xerox art; it was the only student work she could remember from a year of art school. The artist had xeroxed jewellery, old passports; she'd xeroxed a love letter and then dragged it across the scanning plate while it was being copied, so that in the final image the letter was blurred into the shape of a fanned-out deck of cards. The photocopies were blown up and printed onto glass. Kolia couldn't focus on any of them without thinking of the kind of documents that her mother used to bring home: bodies badly photocopied in black and white.

She looks down at Enzo's angelic, thoughtful face.

'Needle, thread, wool, knit,' she says encouragingly.

His eyelashes sweep his cheek. Kolia wonders how boys' faces turn into men's faces. She had sex with Gabriel again last week, whose eyelashes are many and sand-coloured. Gabriel likes doing the trick where he tugs at one corner of his mouth with an invisible string. It makes it look like he's sneering at her, which she finds very sexy. Enzo has recently taken to a similar kind of clowning. He widens his eyes until they're enormous and pouts dramatically and says, in his best baby voice, 'Is this cute? Am I being cute?' It's slightly cute, chiefly unnerving.

'It's knit,' says Enzo now, with confidence.

'Well done! Perfect. Okay, number nine, Enzo. Four children were playing Heads or Tails with a two-pence coin and they scored heads fourteen times. Alex and Ben scored heads the same number of times . . .'

'Do you know why vampires have sharp teeth?' says Enzo.

'No. Now, Alex and Ben scored heads the same number of times. Both Charlie and Daniel scored heads three times—'

'Do you know why vampires have sharp teeth?' says Enzo again, wriggling. 'It's not for eating. It's because they're so old so their teeth have just broken away.'

'Both Charlie and Daniel scored—'

'But people think it's so they can get inside necks and suck blood, but that's not true.'

Kolia presses her lips together in a tight line. She's worried that if Enzo's mother comes home and he's only answered half the questions, she'll lose her job.

'Do you want me to do my work?' Enzo says, perceptively.

'Yes, please.'

'I'll do my work on one condition, if I can scream the whole time.'

He's learned 'on one condition' recently and loves it. Kolia thinks. The parents are out. Devna's gone upstairs, possibly to sit down out of sight. There's a cleaner in the next room who might tell, but she doubts it.

'Okay,' she says. 'Scream.'

Enzo begins immediately. The scream is loud and high-pitched. It is not a single note, which in time might have been possible to tune out. It's varying, almost ululating, but without any of the lightness that one might associate with a child ululating. It's very much a violent scream. He's working through the questions; he's working well. Concentrating on the test isn't sapping the power from his scream. His pauses for breath are bafflingly infrequent. Kolia looks at the time. The kitchen clock is, of course, a reproduction Bruno Munari. Enzo has been screaming for nearly ten minutes. He continues to scream, continues to write. *Leaf is to plant as page is to* . . . The house is big, but some-one must be able to hear. She imagines the cleaner next door with her earphones in and the vacuum on. She imagines Devna, stretched out face-down on the king-size bed in the parents' room, holding a pillow over her head. Enzo raises his head from the question paper and Kolia is looking straight into his mouth. Unplaceable landscapes – caverns, wet rocks, grey-pink corruga-tions in the roof and the teeth shining white and small and bobbly. There's a new tooth sticking up in the left corner of his mouth like a fish hook. The scream gains power. It draws her inside of it until her whole field of vision is filled with the child's screaming mouth. The back gleams filmily and moves.

In the end, Enzo screams for nearly half an hour and gets every question right bar one; by the time the lesson's over Kolia feels like some kind of numbed, ringing carapace has formed around her brain. (The carapace is actually optimal because for a second she'd been on the cusp of another, less controlled reaction. The way his breath was ragged and his jaw hung open like an animal's . . . But just for a second.) 'Great job,' she tells him. Devna lets her out without a word.

The houses get less fancy soon after turning off Enzo's road. By the time she's at the bus stop they're all basically indistinguishable. Screaming aside, Kolia doesn't usually mind spending her afternoons in such a luxurious house. She takes long bathroom breaks, flicks through the magazines they keep in a wicker basket. A wicker basket with gingham lining for their toilet *Home & Gardens*! She wonders what it means that Enzo's mother puts such little drawings in such huge frames. Perhaps she treats her children's artwork as priceless because she loves them so much. Or, perhaps, she's trying to mediate the drawings' unloveliness with big expensive borders that make them look like tiny Twomblys rather than the work of a six-year-old. Kolia has to admit they suit the house better this way.

On the bus, her phone rings in her bag. It stops before she can look at it. When she does, it's a bright column of messages, two screens long, all saying one thing. *Mum's done it again.*

Kolia tips her head back, closes her eyes. Takes a big gulp of air like it's water. She hasn't spoken to Lalita in months. She hasn't seen the boys in as long. The texts are from the oldest boy, her big little brother, saying *she's done it again* and *please come Kolia*. The sense of mounting buzzing duty is on her all at once: parenting a parent, the final word in overdue assignments. She gets off the bus. It's a bright day. Bushes of small, yellow flowers show through the back panels of the bus stop. She gets on another bus.

3.

Kolia's mother lives an hour's drive from London, on a quiet street which runs parallel to the Thames. Every house on her road appears hedge-first. There's a hedge ahead of each front door, or else an elm or a miniature spruce, or some other short, dense tree taking up the whole front yard; green and well-trimmed, without exception. The houses, hedges, street and town are perfectly coherent and their message is peace.

Kolia's mother had wanted to move here for the good of her soul. Kolia thinks that the town's atmosphere (of towpaths, bandstands, open lawns, tennis courts) seems clearly at odds with her mother's soul, which is wild and flashing. But her mother had said she needed to be close to the water. When they'd first moved here, she used to airdry her hair by the river, and sometimes she'd disappear for hours on long walks by the water. Once she told Kolia that whenever she saw a woman on a bike keeping pace with her on the upper bank, she knew it was her guardian angel.

A flash of neon orange on the cycle path. Thistles, black mud, stones. The water high, the sky milky. The poplars pressing in. My mother's out of her depth; the river's brown brooklets are in her eyes and ears. Her clothes are dragging her down faster than the current can drag her along. The guardian angel had been on her way to pick up her ten-year-old son from the Young Mariners' Centre. She sees my mother go under, her T-shirt swelling in the water, ballooning like a plastic bag. With one arm round a fallen tree that overhangs the bank, and then help from a jogger who sees her from the other side of the lock, she saves her. I'm at the hospital by the time my mother wakes up from having her stomach pumped. I'm crying. I haven't seen her in months. 'That water's so dirty,' I say. 'People die just from swimming in it.' My mother takes my hand. She tells me that it's my fault. She only did it because I wasn't talking to her.

That had been four years ago.

'I always meant to write to her,' says Kolia. 'The cyclist lady. Never got round to it.'

'Understandable,' says Mia. 'There was a lot going on.'

Kolia calls Mia every time she has to make this walk; something about the street paralyses her. It's not the destination, it's the street itself – wide windows into perfect front rooms, terracotta planters. A toddler's parked bike leans against one gate, pink-glitter streamers fluttering at the handlebars. She's not sure she'd make it to her mother's house without Mia's voice on the other end of the phone.

'It should be a crime,' Mia's saying. 'That's why they say "commit", you know, because it used to be a crime. Before the nineteenth century, a suicide would be buried at a crossroads with a stake driven through their heart.'

'Yeah,' says Kolia, concentrating on setting one foot down in front of the other. This used to be the way she walked to school.

'And she's a repeat offender,' says Mia.

When I try to cut her out again, my mother drinks bleach. Well, not bleach, but cleaning fluid. Something unbranded and lemon flavoured, stronger than dish soap but softer than Clorox. They pump her stomach to be safe and I come as soon as I hear. 'I just missed you so much,' my mother says, hoarse and sleepy in her white gown. I have nightmares about her insides, scoured and abraded. I have nightmares about her coughing bubbles. I can't scrub a pan without crying.

'The *DSM* calls what she does a suicidal gesture,' says Kolia. 'Self-injury in which there is no attempt to die, only to give the appearance of a suicide attempt in order to communicate with others.'

'I'm looking it up,' says Mia. She hums as she does, so that Kolia won't be left with silence. Mia's gifted at distraction. Her whole way of being is set up to generate a clear image of her on the other end of the phone, and it's the image of a teenager in a 90s movie, taking calls from her bedroom on a heart-shaped handset. A kind of *Clueless* effect, only enhanced by all of her fruit-eating, vitamin-taking prettiness.

'Oh god, yeah, listen,' she says. Kolia imagines her chewing the end of a pencil, winding the cord around her finger until it goes blue. 'Parasuicide, or suicidal behaviour of the "psycho-pathic variety, as a gesture to one's ends".'

She says something unforgiveable. I stop taking her calls. She texts me to say that she's always loved me, that I'll be better off without her, and to tell my brothers that she's moved abroad. 'To Europe,' she says. I call, text, call, try to keep her on the phone while I get to her. She sends a couple of legible messages before the overdose kicks in and the spelling breaks down, a couple of incoherent ones that come through as I tear out of the cab, down her street, past all the awful hedges. I find her passed out in the living room, surrounded by empty blister packs. She's done it, I think. I'm hysterical when the ambulance arrives, only a few minutes later.

We'll keep her for overnight examination, the nurse tells me, but she doesn't need her stomach pumped. I'm very lucky. My mother overdosed on antihistamines.

'She's not dying?' I ask.

'Just drowsy.'

When my mother wakes up, she looks relieved to see me. It's hard to be mad at a woman hooked up to an IV; I guess that's what she banks on, how she wipes the slate clean. My mother nestles dramatically into the hospital bed. Jesus Christ, I want to say, she thinks she's Marilyn on Benzos. I take her hand.

They're nearly here. Or, Kolia is. Mia's fifteen miles away, popping gum in Kolia's ear.

'It says here' – snap – 'that Glenn Close in *Fatal Attraction* has all the ingredients to distinguish a suicide gesture from a suicide attempt, including "a dramatic presentation, the impulsive nature of the act, the choice of method, readily available assistance, and clear cut secondary gain".'

'I haven't seen *Fatal Attraction*,' says Kolia. 'Is that the one where you're supposed to be able to see Sharon Stone's pussy for, like, half a frame when she uncrosses her legs?'

'No, it's the one where she boils the bunny.' Mia pops her gum again. This would be an unpleasant auditory experience except that it's distracted Kolia from the bend in the road which signals the tail end of the journey. '"Parasuicides are more usual in women, especially divorcées. Psychopathy common." I think this article is sexist, you know.'

It doesn't feel like something a psychopath does. It's more desperate than that, rawer, more furious, more pathetic. Sometimes it's 'I'll show you.' Sometimes it's just 'Help me.' I don't ignore her calls any more; I reply to all her texts. But anything can be a perceived

hurt. I go away for three weeks in December and then spend
Christmas with my father. The boys call me on New Year's Day.
She's going to run into traffic, they say, she wants to die again.
When I arrive, my mother's lying in the middle of the road. One
neighbour is threatening to call the police; a boy is watching from a
window, already bored of his presents. My mother is howling, she's
screaming at nothing. Her thighs flash as she rolls over, dimply and
goose-pimpled. She says she's waiting for a car to hit her and then
she sobs. No car will hit her. It's 10 a.m. on New Year's Day and
she's halfway down a residential street that leads into a cul-de-sac.
This isn't the death feint of a psychopath. This is something an
animal does.

'I can see the house,' says Kolia. 'Oh, I feel sick.'

'I hate that you keep having to do this. It's like some twisted
Groundhog Day.'

'Literally. And like, you know how the first time Bill Murray
steps in slush, or gets covered in snow, or sees a kitchen grease
fire—'

'I haven't actually seen *Groundhog Day*,' says Mia. 'But
I've seen *Russian Doll*. And the Groundhog Day *Buffy*
episode.'

'You know what I'm talking about. The first time around,
these are big upsets. But Loop 981, and it's nothing; he skips
the slush, sidesteps the snow, he doesn't even blink at the fire.
I'm Loop 981 of discovering my mother's body.'

'I'd watch that film,' Mia says, and then sighs. 'I don't know
why you still go. Maybe it would be good for her to wake up in
the hospital and realise that it didn't work.'

'According to the *DSM*, the chances of her actually dying
increase every time she tries, even if it's not for real.'

'Fucking hell.'

'But I think that includes accidental success as well. Like if she throws herself out a ground-floor window but twists her ankle and then, like, dies on the operating table.'

'Like a soldier shooting himself in the foot and then accidentally bleeding to death.'

'Right,' says Kolia, distracted. The top of her mother's hedge is in view, two inches taller than the neighbour's yew. 'Oh, Mia, I really don't want to go in. Do you think she'll be chemically coshed?'

'I think she'll have been up all morning tidying the house,' says Mia. 'Or at least since the psych ward released her. She'll be dying to see you.'

Two gates away, the hedge comes into full view. And behind the hedge is No. 25 itself, a house which looks like the houses either side of it. Cream facade, Victorian brickwork, large front window. Intruder alarm at the side. There's dichondra in pots, trailing from the first-floor windows, and a large black trellis standing empty. The front door is inset with two stained-glass panels, one of which is broken and boarded over with tape and cardboard and occasionally lets through tiny fluting drafts that only the dog notices.

'Mia,' says Kolia, very quiet. She'll need to hang up in less than a second, but she isn't ready to let go of the voice on the phone, or to take those last steps over the pinwheel tiles up the front path. 'Do you think – she'll want to talk about it?'

4.

Lalita has been tidying the house all morning. Last night had been a mistake – a horrible muddy rush of screaming, making threats, pounding her forearms on the carpet – but she hadn't really done anything. No psych ward necessary: when the boys threatened to call the police, she'd calmed herself, taken two downers, gone to sleep. She'd woken up in the morning feeling much better and had gone to make it up to them. Archan had sniffled and said sorry, and then admitted that he'd texted Kolia for help less than an hour ago, when he'd thought she was still mad. 'Are you angry?' he'd asked. Angry? Kolia's coming!

She's been tidying for hours. Perhaps if No. 25 is welcoming enough, Kolia will stay the night. It's an odd house, despite looking like its neighbours. Noises in the night, windows at impractical heights, numerous crawl spaces too small for crawling. Strange effluvia from the taps in the summertime. The dirt is odd accordingly. Not more odd than any mess that kids produce, thinks Lalita. Slides from a toy microscope, loose bells, foreign change, capsules: she sorts these into their places without looking. But a line deepens on her forehead at a column of ants crawling from a heap of sand in the corner of the front room, and the kitchen sink is blocked with the grit of broken seashells.

It doesn't help that Lalita's not good at cleaning. She's slow these days. The way that she carries herself is impressive, even stately, but she moves like she's unaccustomed to moving. Worse, she's totally without system. She'll take a cup from the living room table, put it in the kitchen sink, then see a pack of cigarettes by the microwave and walk that to the front room to put in the back of a drawer, and then she'll see a plate on a side table with half a curried mutton sandwich still on it and contemplate shouting up the stairs at whichever boy has left it there, and then she'll decide against that and take the plate to the kitchen sink. Still, by three o'clock she's finished. She puts out a stack of fresh sheets on the console table outside the master bedroom. The master bedroom is always locked, but if Kolia wants to stay, she has a key. Lalita lets her hands fall on the clean sheets, allows herself the quiet of a job well done. She wonders if she'll have a cigarette. Outside, she thinks. Kolia doesn't like the smell.

The living room opens onto the back garden. The unvaried faultlessness of the hedges does not extend here: the lawn's pale and patchy and the dog's dug most of it up into long heaps, the kind left by moles in cartoons. Lalita occupies the doorway in her soft-soled house shoes and lights up. It's 3 p.m.; the sky seems low today. Gold alights here and there on the brambles at the end of the garden, like a quick bird. The blue broken-down shed is full of the sun, the slouching fence around the garden is full of sun. Over the fence, the garden next door is partly visible and it is full of sun too. The doorbell rings. Lalita bends down to stub her cigarette out on the patio and push it through the drain cover. She's smiling as she straightens up.

When the front door opens, Kolia has been staring at the broken pane of glass in it, the terrible mending job of brown package tape, noticing that one leaf of reinforced glass is not secured at all, hanging loose, liable to injure someone, maybe one of the boys, and so she doesn't have time to readjust her face, which means Lalita is met by her full, undisguised judgement.

They don't hug. Lalita looks excited; Kolia tries to make an expression to match, although her gaze has been drawn straight from the glass to a stain on Lalita's sweatshirt. Kolia's wearing a black cotton dress that shows off her brown arms like a tank top.

'You're sweating, dear. Did you run here?'

'It's really hot.'

'I was just in the garden, it seemed okay to me.'

'It's always cool in the garden. It's in the shade of the house.'

'Is it?' Lalita closes her mouth like she's too generous to point out that she's just seen the garden full of sun.

'Yeah, mostly.'

'There are fresh sheets, we've got strawberries, I went and got three six-packs of that water you like . . .'

'Thank you, that's so sweet.' She follows her mother into the house, eyes moving over the clean walls and floors. 'I'm not sure I'm sleeping here.'

Lalita steamrolls on. 'I've bought this really lovely comforter, it's outside your room. I think it's nice just to have soft things.' Silence. 'Do you want a tea? Shall I make you a tea?'

Kolia cringes and leads her mother past the kitchen, into the living room. 'No, no, let's just sit down. How are you feeling? And where are the boys, I wanted to say hi to the boys.'

'Oh, they're upstairs playing. I've been working on a really interesting case actually.'

'But are you – you're okay?'

Lalita ignores the question, relaxing on a couch which Kolia doesn't recognise. Otherwise, the living room looks the same as it did when she had lived here. Same gold wall mirror, same lacquered table, same John Lewis miniature chandelier. She still remembers going with her parents to pick out the fittings, young enough to fall asleep on a display sofa when the lighting department became an overwhelming blaze of cut crystal. Nearly twenty years ago and this room's still the same. Minus her father's books, plus the boys' detritus, plus the couch.

Lalita's describing her current case, which has something to do with the Windrush scandal, and Kolia's asking the follow-up questions that present themselves, when she notices another recent addition to the living room. Unidentifiable on a table, catching the light.

Lalita starts with delight. 'Oh my god, so embarrassing. One of my clients, old client, got me this.' Getting up with some effort, she goes to the side table now cleared of mutton sandwich and takes from it a small cube, shiny, grey or white, which she hands to Kolia.

Kolia's perched on the edge of an ergonomic rocking chair that Lalita bought years ago back when she was nursing one of the boys, possibly the youngest. The tension has not left her body. It's always like this when she first sees her mother again; if Lalita doesn't want to talk about it, Kolia's not going to make her. She looks at the cube politely.

'Basically, he tried to pay me for the case, and I was like look, you've got no money, I'm not charging you, and I won the case, did basically save his life, and two months later he sends me this.'

Lalita looks eagerly for a response. The cube in Kolia's hands is Perspex or Plexiglass, but heavy as if it were crystal. Inside the cube, Lalita's head and shoulders have been 3D printed, etched in white. It's like an inverse Roman bust. Kolia turns it and turns it: her mother at every angle.

'He just used a pic off Google Images. From one of the Muazu solidarity shots, maybe. I think I look quite fierce.'

Whatever photo he used was evidently from a while ago, Kolia thinks. The etched face is alert, sharp, glamorous. The woman on the couch is none of these things, except maybe for her legs and arms, which still have some claim to sharpness. Kolia has watched time soften all of the arresting angles in her mother's face, cheekbones that were once tigerish. However much weight she gains, the limbs stay stick-thin.

'Can I have this?' says Kolia.

'Would you want something like that?' says Lalita, bursting with happiness.

'Yeah, of course.' She turns it, turns it. Long neck, chignon. Sharp nose. The etching almost captures the eyebrow pencil. 'You could really do some damage with this.' She looks up from the etching at her mother, who is staring in undisguised adoration.

'The boys will be so pleased to see you.'

'Oh, I want to say hi now.' Kolia sits up straighter.

'Wait a second,' Lalita says firmly. 'We're all going to do high tea. It's one of the things I've been doing recently. It's good to have rituals. The boys love it.' When Kolia doesn't look convinced, she narrows her eyes. 'They asked you to come and check on me, didn't they? *I* need you first.'

Kolia pushes her toes against the floor, sets the nursing chair rocking a little. Her eyes track her mother's movements. Lalita digging in a handbag, finding a vape. 'Is that the cotton candy one?' Kolia says.

'Yes. My breathing's been tight since last week, so I've been really good about only vaping.'

'That's good. Trouble breathing since last week?'

'On and off. I've been finding the stairs more difficult since I had the' – she gestures vaguely at her stomach – 'everything removed.' Lalita's referring to a routine gallstones operation that she had a month ago. Once the parasuicides have been swept under the carpet, her less severe medical emergencies become the go-to points of reference. (Kolia had met her father for lunch the other day and he'd said, gravely calculating over chicken, that he wouldn't be surprised if there'd never been a surgery, or even any gallstones at all.)

'You taking all your meds?' Conversational. The chair rocks.

Lalita exhales a thin horn of cotton candy. 'Yes. And I've had a lot of stress recently, billing, and the boys don't pick up after themselves, but what I've been doing when I'm really stressed is taking these over-the-counter hay fever tablets that just knock you out. Which is actually much better for me than the diazepam, which is what I was taking before.'

'Okay. I don't know if that's good.'

She nods enthusiastically. They're so good, she tells Kolia, that sometimes the older boy takes them when *he* can't get to sleep.

'What?' Kolia lowers her voice. 'You can't give him sleeping pills. He's like fourteen.'

'But he gets really anxious. And if he can't sleep then he doesn't go to school. He's hardly there at all at the moment. Plus they're for hay fever – teenagers take them all the time.'

Kolia turns the cube over. The anxiety is a manageable thrum in her throat. She decides to change the subject. 'How's Ammama?'

Ammama, meaning mother's mother. Kolia's dad refers to the woman in question as Ammamamamama but Kolia doesn't see anything funny about this, an invocation of her mother's mother's mothers cycling back unstoppably.

'She's doing really well,' says Lalita. 'Loving on the Orphans, as usual. I FaceTimed her the other day and a parrot picked up the phone! A red macaw.'

'Did it?' Kolia scans her for obvious insanity – twitching, talking too fast, scratching (which is her worst habit), but Lalita's stretched out on the couch, smiling at her daughter, totally normal.

'You like the couch?' she asks with pleasure, misunderstanding Kolia's attention. 'It's new.'

She found it on eBay, she explains. It's actually an antique. It used to belong to a colonial outpost in the country where Lalita was born.

Lalita's side of the family is from an island country, which has gone by various names, many of which mean 'island'. It was first famous as a pearl trading kingdom. It's still known for its pearls, as well as its beaches and human rights violations, and is thought to be the birthplace of the oldest surviving language in the world. An ancient poet described the island as being ruled first by nature-spirits, and later by demons: it has since been colonised by the Portuguese, the Dutch and the English. Shortly after its independence from the last of these, laws were passed which discriminated against the island's minority population. Violence and persecution followed, then insurgency, then twenty-six years of civil war. The civil war ended more than ten years ago, but its effect has lasted. Lalita's family left just before war broke out. Now her mother has returned to watch over the Orphans and the red macaws.

'I really love the idea that some dead white official is rolling in his grave at that fact that I'm sitting on it now, eating crisps.' Lalita gestures to the couch arms, taps the wood. It has a four-poster frame for hanging a canopy. 'They had to move around all the time, depending on where they were posted, right, so the couch completely disassembles. Means shipping cost almost nothing.'

Kolia looks out at the garden. Pampas grass grows from the side of the broken blue shed, with thistles at knee height. She doesn't like to go in the garden when she comes to visit. It had been boundless and wild when Kolia was little, a tangled domain that she had governed as farmer, witch, archer, ghost. She could have lived for a summer off the blackberries that multiplied in the damp black space behind the shed. Now she finds the garden small and tame, with all its colours turned down.

'Where's the dog?'

Lalita doesn't seem to hear her. 'Ammama's still asking when you're going to come out, visit the school. She says you're turning into a—' Lalita uses the word which in her mother's language means white person. Technically, it means white man. White Guy, capital W, capital G. 'How's your father, speaking of?'

Kolia wishes that Sheba were here. She doesn't love dogs, but this would usually be her cue to lower her eyes and pet something. The way Lalita talks about Kolia's father is so weird. Lightly, with a sympathetic understanding. As though the divide between them is incidental rather than deeply rooted and deeply felt, with deep-running ramifications. Once, she'd talked fondly about how he'd always forgotten her birthday. 'Maybe that's why we're not together,' she'd said, pensive.

When Kolia thinks of them together, the images are sweet. He combs Lalita's hair out, he leads Kolia in making her mother a birthday cake. She doesn't understand how these things could ever have come to pass, but that's what she remembers, which she imagines is largely down to the efforts of her father. But then you'd have Mum in the spare room, intense and unfocused, telling secrets and packing her bags.

'Dad's good. He's been doing some guest lecturing in Munich.'

Agreeably, Lalita starts back up with the work talk. She's deep in case talk when she pauses to fart, long and low, on the colonial couch. 'My guts aren't right,' she says. 'I'm being gaslit.'

Kolia almost smiles. When she'd first introduced her mother to the word 'gaslighting', Lalita's head nearly fell off from laughing. The stupidest thing she'd ever heard, she'd said: a new word for the oldest thing in the world. That's just how men are, darling.

Now, it's happening at her chambers. Talk of disbarment, claims that Lalita is unfit to practise. It's called whistleblowing, she'd explained virtuously. She'd written to a journalist about the treatment of a client who'd been in detention: the client's health had been in critical condition; the detention centre wouldn't allow him to receive medical care. The journalist had reported her for sharing confidential information. And now all of chambers is in on it, together, trying to crush her. Kolia refuses to get involved. It's hard to make sense of her mother's reports of men – bureaucrats – who want to get her in trouble just for being such an amazing lawyer! Kolia abides by the *Believe Women* dictum, of course. But her mother is often hard to believe.

'You know what,' Kolia says, and throws the tea back. 'I'll bring the boys down here.'

5.

The boys are playing a game in the dichondra room. Archan is sat in a purple gaming chair, controlling the movements of a pixelated Wood Elf. The Baby's at his elbow, helping to direct.

When Kolia enters, they turn the computer off. Both boys awkwardly hug her; both are beaming.

'You didn't have to turn it off for me,' she says.

Do you like that game? they ask. Do you like this other game? Do you know about the alternative ending? Did you hear about this modification? I found a whole new land behind the Stones of Barenziah. I found—

Kolia laughs and enthuses back about the video game, displaying a patchy and erroneous knowledge put together from boys she's dated and kids she's tutored. It's hard for her not to play the expert with them. The boys let her mistakes pass, nodding eagerly, happy she's there.

She wanders the room like an inspector, letting her hand fall on a forgotten cup, checking the elbow of a school jumper. It had been a study when she lived here. She'd learned to spell in this room, looking out at the quiet road and all its hedges from the dichondra window, though there hadn't been dichondra then. It had been in this room (looking out at the quiet road and all its hedges) that she'd realised the hedges were only paint-strokes, and then that she'd realised she needed glasses, which had struck her at the time as a tragic injustice and life-changing disability, though she's only ever been a little short-sighted. Kolia doesn't bother with her glasses now, partly out of vanity and partly because she likes the way the world spreads out at her – gently, impressionistically, filmy landscapes of suggestion rather than detail. A baby's eyes don't focus properly until two months after birth. This is so they can understand all the new things they encounter rather than immediately becoming lost to a maze of detail: pores, hairs, sclera, cilia. Without glasses, Kolia's gaze lands on what is significant and identifiable. In this house, her eyes are attracted to dirt. She's trained to catch it. (A housecoat, belonging to her mother, hangs on the back of the door. She puts her fingers into its pockets, finds an empty vape. Rolls her eyes, hard.)

'You guys are wanted downstairs for tea.'

The Baby throws himself on the bed dramatically.

'We're doing high tea all the time now,' Archan explains. 'It just means Mum gets really mad if we don't eat any of the biscuits, and we can't have hot chocolate or milk or anything, it has to be tea.'

'I don't even like tea,' says the Baby, incredulous.

'She's NUTS,' they say. 'She's crazy.'

Kolia exhales. 'What actually happened last night?'

'She was being crazy but then she went to sleep and she was normal. But I thought . . .' Archan twists his fingers together, 'I thought you should come. Just in case. Because when you're here, it's better.'

'You did the right thing,' says Kolia. She isn't sure that there is a right thing any more, exactly, but it's true that they couldn't have done anything else. 'I'll try not to stay away so long, okay?' She closes her eyes for just enough time that they look at her strangely and then she claps. 'Let's get going.'

*

They eat in the front room. The shortbread is fanned out on a plate, one yellowish finger after another. Lalita's sitting at the head of the table, smiling beatifically as though to say that she doesn't mind having waited for them. Kolia hasn't been in this front room for a long time. The tabletop is a pane of glass, beneath which she can see the boys poking each other. She looks up from the shortbread, and from her brothers' knobbly knees, and out at the hedge. It's trimmer than she remembers. Sparser.

She remembers being small beneath it. She'd run away from home and not made it past the front garden. This must have been eighteen, nineteen years ago. She had crouched in the gravel so that no one standing in the front room could spot her. It was a good memory, gleeful; getting past the front door was a success. She'd hidden behind the hedge for seeming hours with another fugitive, a little Italian boy called Nino, who was her best friend. They'd shared out the provisions, and rang the bell sheepishly as soon as it got dark. Lalita had appeared at the front window, imperious and elegant in the way that she used to be, and made them wait another two hours before opening the door, to teach them a lesson. Those two hours are printed on Kolia's brain, though what happened afterwards is a blur.

It's strange to be back in this room. When her parents lived here together, this was where the family ate every meal. Now Lalita and the boys eat in the kitchen mostly, although apparently they've resurrected this space for some kind of regular high tea. Kolia guesses that her mother stopped using the front room because the tracks of her past life are entrenched too deeply here. All the ghostly circuits of living here the first time round; the same glass table that her first husband laid for her first child's breakfast. Not that the front room used to look like this. There was never shortbread fanned out on porcelain plates when Lalita was home the first time.

In fact, where now there is a tall, many-drawered medicine cabinet, also thrifted from the colonials, there had once been a message written on the wall in red lipstick. Kolia can't remember what it said, but she remembers showing Nino the swear words in it. (She'd shown him shyly, like when you try to make a boy laugh with the smooth plastic crotch of your favourite doll and then feel instant regret at having violated something sacrosanct. Princess Anneliese would never look at you the same way again.) She remembers Nino tracing the red, smeared words with his finger. A message from her mother to her father. And then Lalita rising, shouting, Get out, Kolia, I'm working. Black-and-white photocopies of photographs of bodies on the glass tabletop. She didn't tell Nino to get out; no one could see him except Kolia.

'Do you like the tea?' says Lalita. 'Ceylon, with a little honey.'

'It's so good, Mum,' the boys chorus obediently; Kolia nods too.

The Baby asks Kolia a question about red macaws but forgets that he wants an answer after Archan makes it clear that they have to get back to their game.

'No games,' says Lalita sharply, and they sit down at once. 'Your sister's here. If you're naughty, she'll never ever come again.'

Kolia winces. 'I actually have to go.'

Lalita looks heartbroken but she swallows her tongue until she's able to say, 'Such a drive-by,' and sound somewhat chirpy.

'I'll be back.' Kolia looks at Archan. 'I promise.'

Kolia takes her plate back to the kitchen. She moves quietly, manoeuvres around all the evidence of Sheba: an empty bowl, the smell and the wet insides of food tins. She's not much for dogs, really. There's a metal tray on top of the microwave which holds five gods. Conch, club, lute, skull, skin, bell: all the hand-held totems in the same wash of brass. With one eye on the door, Kolia pulls out a wicker drawer. Asthma meds, anti-depressants, an antibiotic treatment for the latest apparent ailment. She rifles through the bottles and blister packs with two fingers until she finds a small bottle of Vyvanse, which she puts in her pocket.

On her way out, she pokes her head through the door of the front room, where the boys are still detained in front of a half-full plate of shortbread.

'Bye, love you,' says Kolia. They all watch her leave. She'd stayed less than thirty minutes.

6.

At the top of her mother's road, Kolia turns left, carefully not looking in the direction of the riverside park. She walks towards the town centre, making loops to avoid the dark antique store, the novelty sweetshop, the haberdashery done up to look ye olde, all the dear little places that shore up that particular air: of towpaths and bandstands, of the lock-keeper's brutal cottage. She ducks instead into the department store at the heart of the town. The outside is all old gold stone, crests carved around tall windows, but the inside's the same as any shopping centre. It's quiet. A crisp packet caught in the escalator flutters sadly on Kolia's way to the third floor.

When Kolia was eleven, a woman had jumped to her death from this floor, over the railing just outside the Zara. She'd fallen through the central plaza of the mall in front of hundreds of shoppers. 'She must have really wanted people to see,' Lalita had said. Kolia wonders if the Baby is old enough to come here with his friends after school. She hopes he doesn't know that story.

The cafés up here are already shuttered; someone has graffitied fruit-women on the rolling gates: pears with tits, apples mouthing obscenely. Some delayed reaction to the afternoon is playing out in her lungs. Deflatedness and deferred panic, combining in a sort of charged deadness.

Kolia walks in circles outside the Zara. The tiles will have been replaced since she was eleven, she supposes. She stops right by the railing, takes out her phone, hovers over Gabriel's contact. Before she presses his name, she looks down over the edge. She can see a fountain three floors down, shallow, under-lit, the sort for throwing coins in. She calls him.

The phone rings a dozen times, which makes sense. They've never called before; they're not on calling terms. Only sleeping together terms. Thinking about his eyelashes at work terms. Mia doesn't understand what Kolia sees in him at all. They'd first met Gabriel as a school friend of Fillipo, Mia's homemade-bandana-wearing ex, and in Mia's phases of disenchantment with Gabriel, she would insist that the two were unbearably alike, lazy and entitled. Generally Mia likes Gabriel, in an indulgent, unconcerned sort of way, but she always says that Kolia must really be putting the work in to get anything else out of him. And it's true that Kolia's caught herself before, studying all his terrible freelance articles for clues of his brilliance, flashes of genius in 'Five Historical Figures Who Were On Drugs The Whole Time' or 'Six Times The Kennedy Curse Was Real And One Time It Was Just Terrible Parenting'. It's not her fault, Mia says; in the twentieth century, we got rid of God and put the mother in his place, and now in the twenty-first, Kolia's been forced to make a second substitution. ('But if you're gonna get your love and your tenderness and your authority from somewhere that's not God and that's not Lalita, I just don't know why you'd pick *Gabe*.') Kolia doesn't have an answer. Still, when he picks up the phone, the heaviness in her lungs recedes.

She looks around the mall while they talk. The five-o'clock gloom pressing in at the skylight, *Dream Cloud* written in neon pastels on the vape stall. No one around but the store assistants and the guy with the popcorn cart, an old man in black head-phones. Gabriel doesn't have Mia's trick of sounding like she's made for idle phone calls. Kolia can feel him wondering why she's called. She makes a gambit, eyes on the neon sign.

'You were in my dream last night.'

'Oh yeah?' She hears Gabriel shift, pictures him stretching, settling in, but when he asks her for details she can't continue.

In fact, her dreams have been full of him, but not in any easily sexy way, not in ways that lend themselves to telling. She puts mice into a paper shredder and is scared to empty out the pink slime; he does it for her and they kiss. Or he reveals that he has a fetish for crushing girls under his reclining car seat. Or he asks Kolia if she's mad at him because he'd been mean about her imaginary friend and she tells him that she'd never be mad over something imaginary. Dreams of his mother's house, a dark green garden covered in a thin layer of snow, he's lost weight. She passes him on a trail path and they nearly don't stop; he says it felt good to walk past her and that he wouldn't have turned around but the weather made him. In the most recent dream, he whispers that he's in love with her, almost inaudible, then leans back on his elbows and waits for her to say it too.

The pause begins to strain. It's always like this; she can't ever play it cool. Kolia tries to put away the instinct as soon as it arrives, but it's too late. She needs softness from Gabriel now, needs to hear care in his voice.

'I've had a really hard day,' she hears herself say. The change in her own inflection revolts her. 'My mum – my little broth-ers . . .' Kolia can't stop it, the rush of recent misfortunes, soft lures, bright and spineless. She wonders if it feels like this for Lalita, if the gallstones stick in her throat before they come out.

'That sounds grim,' says Gabriel. Already she can hear him preparing to disengage. Two more platitudes and an excuse. In her head, his thumbs are twitching over a console, or he's making a face at the rest of a group: guys, I'm trying to hang up.

The fountain glows up at her from three floors below. A layer of wishing coins shifts dreamily over green tile. The coins sing underwater, in her mother's voice. *It's your fault,* they sing. *I only did it because you're not talking to me.*

7.

Kolia had first met Mia through a boy at art school. This was Mia's ex, Gabriel's friend: the boy who had called himself Fillipo, though he was really a Phillip, and who'd been known around campus for cutting odd bits of cloth into strips and tying them round his forehead in a piratical way. Theirs was that sort of group. Portuguese soukous and Ukrainian playing cards, for example, at the party where Mia was first introduced, only no one knew any games that worked with a deck of thirty-six cards, so everyone was just passing them around appreciatively. But then Mia arrived, dauntlessly cheerful, perching on a sofa arm and suggesting that they play beer pong instead.

Mia hadn't gone to the art school; she was studying theology. She told everyone that she knew too little about art to discuss it, that she was a committed devotee of low culture – 'And not reworked either, none of that Basquiat does *The Simpsons* shit.' But despite her apparent disinterest, and despite her relationship with Fillipo, it soon became clear that she had a perfect nose for anything hacky or trite, which (in combination with her actual perfect nose) drew Kolia in immediately.

Kolia's student workrooms were housed in a Victorian building near an intersection that led to the city's main park, a big stretch of limestone downland. Roadkill in abundance: a spilled hare; a flattened lizard; once, somehow, a bat. Fillipo was one of many who put the roadkill in his art. Mia laughed every time, even at one piece that Kolia thought more or less worked: a sparrow whose corpse made the exact shape of an edematous human heart, its little beak tucked against its steamrolled breast like an open valve. But Kolia laughed at it too – how could she not? Mia's teasing was perfect, scornless, true. It made a club of the two of them.

('Ah, not another taxidermied crucifixion.'

'Not another rat in doll's underwear.'

'Oh, life in death, you say?')

Often, Kolia felt untethered in the draughty Victorian work-shops, surrounded by other art students, all of whom seemed to have a clarity of vision, of artistic ambition. Her flatmate was regularly away, pitching 'Girl with a Snail in Her Lung' to the-atres in Soho. It was a relief to be around Mia. She radiated a kind of undirected contentedness, and, not following any particular star, to Soho or otherwise, regularly stumbled into strange, singular situations. When this happened, Fillipo liked to act as if that was Mia's artistic practice – collecting experiences. Mia, of course, would laugh.

It was one of these odd bottle-episode incidents that had truly inaugurated their friendship. Not long after Mia's debut at the soukous party, she'd asked if Kolia would help her out with a 'work thing'. She was always getting crazy messages online about her prettiness, her perfect nose and no-make-up lashes, whether someone could see the shadow of her nipple and so on. One man had said that he would pay five hundred pounds just to rub sun cream into her back. She could choose the place, he'd said; she could even bring her own sun cream. Would Kolia come along and watch from a distance, make sure nothing mad happened?

It was not an erotic afternoon. Too cloudy for sun cream, really, and Mia had picked out a middlingly public spot on the downs, not far from the roadkill junction. All the birds surreally unflattened. Kolia had been sat on a towel a little way off, close enough to see the man walk past Mia, double back, walk past again, and then finally introduce himself. Close enough to hear Mia say, 'Can I just grab the money first, do you think?' and then, 'Okay, nothing any further round the side than here and nothing any further down than here.'

Mia had lain on her stomach and the man had knelt at her side, not astride her, as Kolia had feared he might. He'd poured half the sun cream into his big red hand. Then he'd started spreading it – not on her back – in her hair, pushing it into her scalp and under her braids.

Mia had started screaming. Kolia had leapt up, screaming too, and charged towards the man, spraying her pocket deodorant in front of her. He'd fled with surprising quickness, leaving both the girls still screaming in the downs, Mia covering herself as she stood up.

'That was crazy,' she'd said. 'I didn't even think about my hair.' She was breathing loud, forcefully slow. Kolia saw the flicker in her throat and knew it was the effort of not letting all the breath come out of her at once.

'If Fillipo calls this art, I'll kill him for you,' she'd promised.

Unstoppable closeness that year, a fountain. In spite of her apparent aversion to art, Mia was perfect for Kolia's partnered course projects. Emotional mapping. Body-clock recalibration. One performance workshop had set a task where pairs took turns speaking on a single topic for ten minutes without hesitation – birds or colours or water – the catch being that they weren't allowed to relate the topic to themselves at all. Kolia's prompt had been houses. Mia had struggled, starting with some patchy theorising about making a house a home, leaving obvious gaps where she'd cut herself off, and eventually drifting into using a general, impersonal pronoun to obscure what was clearly specific and personal. For example: 'One might say that they were going to spend a whole night on the trampoline in a sort of leaving-home bid for independence, but if one is still able to look into the kitchen window from the trampoline and see one's mother looking back, their having left home is debatable.' Or 'Perhaps use and wear is what makes a house a home – a nail-varnish drawing on the wall of one's doll, or a weird texture from one's brother melting iron-on patches onto the carpet . . .'

Kolia, on the other hand, had excelled. ('A house is a building designed for habitation. A house is a private space, defined in relation to the outside, or public . . .')

'How are you finding this so easy? I've heard you bring your mother into a conversation about Real Madrid.'

'I like taking myself out of stuff too,' Kolia had said. 'When it comes to school stuff – when it comes to art, I mean. I like to be removed from the output.' That's why she liked process-heavy pieces, where there was an intercessor between her and the work – a printing press or a sewing machine. Or collaging found objects: newsprint from before she was born, photographs of other people. In her sculpting module, which she hadn't enjoyed, she'd preferred materials that wouldn't hold the marks of her fingers. Cloth and wire, she'd explained to Mia, rather than plaster and clay.

'That's crazy.' Mia hadn't been teasing, but her seriousness was somehow worse. 'If I were you, I'd put myself in all my art. Look.'

And she'd sketched Kolia while they sat there, quickly but carefully. It was a bad drawing but Kolia had been able to see what

Mia had meant by it. She'd been able to see herself as Mia had meant: dark hair, dark eyes, eyebrows that still wanted to meet in the middle, like the wings of a bird. Intense, but not as skulking as she sometimes feared; sharp, but not mean. Pretty, even.

PART 2: AMMAMA

2004

Kolia is six years old. She has a wide, round face and eyebrows that meet in the middle like the wings of a bird and she hates being in trouble – she starts to cry the moment that Mr Thompson says he'll be having a word with her parents. Normally Mr Thompson is one of the best teachers; he made pancakes in assembly once, on Shrove Tuesday. But he looks very stern as he walks her out into the playground after school and he gestures to the giants standing about in the autumn leaves. 'Which one's your mummy?'

Kolia points out a man in a mackintosh, waiting at the side of the see-saw. As soon as they're close, she runs into his arms. She stays tucked into her father's side, doesn't dare look at his face when Mr Thompson asks him to please come back to the classroom. She holds his hand all the way down the corridors, which empty out and then are suddenly ghostly. The smell of wet coats floats in the bare cloakrooms; a caretaker vacuums the carpet under the Year 5 self-portraits. At last her father sits down on a blue plastic classroom chair. He has a magic normalising power for which Kolia is often grateful. When she's older, she'll recognise the power for what it is: brilliant, Victorian decorum, capable of turning any room into a lecture hall over which he presides and currently reducing Mr Thompson back to his gentle, pancake-flipping self.

'I doubt that Kolia understands the gravity of this situation,' Mr Thompson is saying, and then, less kindly, 'but it's really unacceptable. Having material of this nature in a school environment makes for serious upset.' He slides Kolia's maths homework across the desk. 'It's on the back.'

On the back is a photocopied image of someone's arm.

Kolia doesn't understand why she's in trouble. She didn't understand in the morning when Mr Thompson had stared at her maths in the homework tray and then whipped it furiously away. Her mum had given her the scrap paper for her answers, and it looked like most of their scrap paper: arms, legs, hands, chests; black-and-white pictures that her mother brought home from work. But her father is nodding, grave and reassuring, saying that he understands completely and that nothing like this will ever be brought into school again.

Usually they play games on the walk home from school, like One Elephant Two Bananas, or the one where every paving stone's a country and they leap around the world. Today her father marches ahead and Kolia struggles to keep up. The river's high; the magpies rattle. On the home stretch, the smell of rain in hedges. Just as her dad turns the key in the lock, the woman next door comes out. She isn't taking the bins out or anything, just standing in her front garden watching them over the wall. Her bright red hair draws all the colour out of the cold air – her face is white, like there's a layer of chalk over it. Kolia pulls her hands into her sleeves. Her father nods politely, raising his eyebrows in a way that says *can't talk, short for time, aren't we all?* with a perfect neighbourly wryness.

It's warm at home; Kolia feels better almost instantly. Her father helps her with her shoes and sends her to her room to change. She can sense from the stairs the exact moment that he thumps down on the sofa with a sigh. They don't talk about the arm on her maths homework when she comes back down; she finishes *Badgers in the Basement* and he tells her to stop doodling in her reading record.

They're eating dinner when her mother gets back. The front room blooms with perfume before she has opened the door. Kolia's fascinated by her mother's perfumes, which she keeps in coloured bottles on a silver tray and which look better than they smell – like pale wines and potions.

'Darling,' says her mother. 'How was school?'

'Have you eaten, Lalita?' her father interrupts. 'Why don't you join me in the kitchen.'

They leave Kolia with the invisible cloud of perfume. She pushes the pasta around her plate, looks down at her knees through the glass tabletop. It's dark outside: the hedge that separates their house from the street is a block of black. The voices coming from the kitchen are raised. Gritted-teeth voices. She jumps down off her chair and takes her plate out.

Her dad looks monstrous. 'Sit down, Kolia. I've been explaining what Mr Thompson said.' Kolia sits on the stool in the corner. Her mother has her back to both of them; she's reorganising fruit in the bowl on the counter.

'The clients that your mother represents often need to prove that they have been injured.'

'Tortured,' says her mother to the peaches.

'So, they take photographs of their injuries. Apparently, your mother has been giving you scrap paper with photocopies of these photographs on. Well, sometimes they're photocopies. Sometimes the clients will scan their wounds into the photocopier directly. Like when you make copies of your hands. It's easier to annotate straight onto that.'

Kolia nods. She loves going to her mother's chambers and has learned how to photocopy her own hands for when her mum's busy; she likes waiting for the beep and the printout, which always looks like all the fuzzy black-and-white photocopies of limbs that her mother brings home, and then she likes to draw rings and long painted nails on the paper hand with highlighters. Her mother wears lots of rings, and always has perfect dark nails.

'The picture on your maths sheet was a fourth-degree burn. It's not appropriate to take these images into school, or to use them as scrap paper at all. We don't want you to be looking at pictures of where people have been hurt.'

'Where they've been beaten,' says her mother, turning around very suddenly. Her mouth is sharp and mean; her voice is so hard, so sing-song with spite, that Kolia starts crying again but Lalita doesn't stop talking. 'Beaten, or struck with a pipe or a spiked baton.' Kolia's crying because her mother sounds so angry but now she's crying at all these new words too, these awful-sounding words that can happen to someone's arm. 'Or whipped, or burned with an iron. Mr Thompson doesn't think you should know that these things happen. So you can use printer paper from now on.'

'For God's sake,' her father roars.

That night he has to read almost all of *Hamster in a Hamper* before Kolia can fall asleep.

2005

When Kolia moves up from Infants to Juniors, her school uniform polo shirt is exchanged for a proper (poly)cotton blouse. She strokes the new fabric on her sleeves and pretends that she's dressing up for court. She has to wear tights now too and these make her feel even more like her mother. Sometimes she actually steals her mother's lacy pantyhose, shivering in the sheer Lycra at the breakfast table until somebody notices that they're falling off her.

Her mother's court clothes have their own closet: silk shirts, pencil skirts, spotless barrister bibs. They share the mirror on court mornings: Kolia brushes her teeth while her mother does her make-up in thick Bollywood swipes. She says it has to go on thick for it to stand out under the horsehair wig. Before she gets in her taxi, she tells her daughter who she will be channelling in court that day: 'I want to be Morgan le Fay today,' or 'I want to be Kali.' Boudicca. Rani of Jhansi. Storm from X-Men.

('Who's Morgan le Fay?' Kolia asks her father on the way to school.)

Kolia still gets excited at half term and on occasional weekends when her mother brings her along to chambers. All the clerks say she's getting big. She fiddles with the desk toys and pretend to answer calls – 'Working on the first set of grounds now, skeleton will be ready in an hour' – and then follows the clicks of her mother's heels over the mossed stone paths of the inns of court to Pret A Manger. Possibly the joy is feeling that, through her mother, she has a claim to this world: the libraries, chapels, stone halls and secret gardens, the antique dust and the gold-lettered ranks of ledgers. And her mother loves to share. She talks to Kolia like she's an adult: she tells her all about her new case, a little boy called Nino.

Nino's father had been in the rebel militia since the beginning of the war. He's missing or dead now, wanted by the government. (Kolia nods wisely, both hands round her Pret hot chocolate. She pretends she's drinking a cappuccino.) Nino's mother had travelled illegally to Sicily, where she'd given birth to Nino. Nino loved Palermo. He didn't know any other home; he'd never been to the island country. He played football on the beach and did well in school and had lots of friends. Some of his friends' parents had grown up with his: lots of people from the island had fled to Sicily. When he was seven, Nino's mother decided that he would be better off in the UK, because she still didn't have leave to remain in Italy. She sent him to live with an uncle in Hertfordshire. But first, she burned him all over his back and shoulders with cigarettes.

'As evidence of state torture, you see? She wanted to provide proof that Nino needed asylum in the UK and couldn't be sent back to his parents' home country.' Lalita leans in, eyes bright with the punchline. 'But what she hadn't realised was that because Nino was born in Italy, he's already a legal citizen there, which also makes him automatically entitled to legal UK citizenship. Regardless of his status. He could have hopped on a plane at any time.'

'Oh my gosh,' Kolia says, to show she understands. Her heart feels sort of folded-over.

It turns out that Nino's uncle in Hertfordshire has two teen-age daughters, neither of whom appreciate the new arrival. They called up an immigration enforcement hotline to report the cigarette scam. Now the Home Office are contesting whether Nino was born in Italy at all. Kolia's mother is leaving for the state archives in Palermo next week to find a registry of his birth.

The house is quiet when she goes. Since Kolia's been in junior school, the gritted-teeth voices have graduated into shouting, and the shouting matches have become more frequent and are no longer restricted to the kitchen. Her dad plays with her every day while her mother's in Sicily: Sleeping Queens and Ludo and Land vs Sea; he copies out pictures for her to colour with such care that Kolia can't tell the difference between his Mona Lisa and the one in the book. Tonight they were painting little clay dinosaurs that go in the oven. But at dinnertime when she asks when Mum's coming back, he shakes his head like he can't be bothered to think about it.

'She just wants a free holiday,' he says.

Kolia blows into her water glass.

'No,' he continues, talking louder as he warms to his theme. 'No, she wants to run around Palermo pretending she's a spy. She wants to act out her heroic fantasies. The thing about your mother is that she does not live in reality. She lives in this completely imaginary picture of herself. This is just the Lalita show: Palermo episode. I'm sorry but it's true.'

That night, Kolia can't sleep. She's all alone on the first floor; her parents sleep upstairs. The master bedroom is down the hall from her, but it stands empty. It scares Kolia sometimes, the master bedroom: an unknown quantity, undusted, unvisited. It's always locked. She wriggles in bed, stretches her feet out towards the corners of the cold single sheet. There's a fireplace in her room, an Art Deco iron one from when the house was built at the end of the nineteenth century, which has never been lit as long as they've lived here. It lets all the warmth out instead, makes the room cold like iron. Kolia gets up and pads softly to the window. She can see the neighbour's back yard: black rectangle, silver glint of planters, the shadow of palm spikes. It's scary, only because it's where the woman with red hair and the chalk-face lives. There's a husband too, a giant with dreadlocks, but he's not scary; he's hardly there anyway. Kolia lets the blinds fall and gets back into bed. She doesn't understand what her dad meant about the Lalita show, and she misses her mother. Most days Lalita goes out early and gets home late anyway but it's strange and sad not to see her at all, even if she has gone to Palermo to save a little boy.

Nino's the same age as Kolia. ('I have to go and help him,' Lalita had said, instead of goodbye. 'He's the same age as you.') He's out in the dark countryside somewhere, waiting for help. His father might be dead; his mother's hurt him and his cousins have betrayed him.

Alone, awake, Kolia thinks about the little boy until he comes to life.

Kolia's Nino is modelled closely on the real thing. He's her age; he loves football and the beach; he has cigarette burns across his back and shoulders. Kolia and Nino tell each other everything. Sometimes his father shows up and tries to recruit him to the militia and they have to run away together. Sometimes they join up of their own accord, to fight injustice. Sometimes, she's another ward of his uncle. In this world she's the first person Nino meets when he arrives in England and she comforts him when he's hurt and suspicious; together, they defeat his horrible cousins. Occasionally she translates him into a completely unrelated scenario, like they have to charter separate competing pirate ships. Even when this happens, she often finds that he has wounds which need tending across his back and shoulders.

Now when her parents fight at night, Nino gets under the covers with Kolia and holds her hand until she falls asleep. The fights have been worse, lately. Kolia's father is increasingly critical of Lalita's heroic fantasies, which have recently manifested as offering strangers a room for a week and giving lifts to hitch-hikers. Fine, except that it's Kolia's room, and it's Kolia in the back of the car going halfway to Oxford when she's meant to be getting dropped off at school.

Nino and Kolia get good at identifying the exact tenor which identifies the graduation of a neutral statement into a declaration of war. They get good at staring at the fireplace until the iron flowers shimmer. Kolia's glad when her mother starts sleeping on a mattress in the study, because she's just started getting nightmares again and now there's a parent down the hall, but then Lalita gets in the habit of staying out for days at a time. When she does come home, she gets straight into bed, and Kolia goes to tuck her in, comfort her, brush her hair out. She learns to be an excellent sounding board. It feels very adult, being entrusted with her mother's secrets; it feels like listening to case files over Pret.

For a while, Kolia's able to lean into her role, as if the battles of No. 25 are just a real-life extension of the pirates-and-soldiers scenarios she invents with Nino. She interrupts one roaring fight in the kitchen to stand between her parents, arms spread out like a Sabine, imploring them not to argue with a series of stock tragic phrases, passionately delivered. And when her teacher has the class do a worry circle, Kolia says, 'I'm worried my parents are going to get divorced' in a little half whisper, because she needs to beat Olivia Gadwall, who's worried that her dog's going to die. She gets assigned lunchtime counselling with Mrs Fallada soon after.

Mrs Fallada asks Kolia which character on the Tree she feels like. The Tree is a poster in her office, with faceless cartoon men doing different things around it. One man's watering the Tree, one's hiding in a treehouse, one's climbing up to get an apple, and so on. Every lunch, Nino points to the faceless man sawing off the branch that he's sitting on. Every lunch, Kolia ignores him and points to the one on the tyre swing. The Tree is cool, like a doll's house or a diorama. Mrs Fallada's cool too, because before she was a teacher she'd been famous for playing the little girl sweeping the stage at the beginning of *Les Mis*. At home, Kolia's tiring of her own role. Lalita's started breaking plates, and whenever they argue, she says that Kolia's her father's daughter.

One day, Kolia and Nino pretend to run away. They don't make it past the front garden, but stay crouched in the gravel so that no one standing in the front room can spot them. The hedge for the house next door is wild and thick, something a witch would put around a tower. Maybe the chalk-faced lady is a witch, Nino says. It feels like they're hiding for a long time; they whisper and break into laughter and wish they'd packed something to read. But nobody comes to look for them so they ring the doorbell sheepishly as soon as it starts to get dark. There's no response. Kolia rings the bell again and peers through the stained-glass window in the door, trying to make out movement, but everything's still. She panics for a moment before something red appears in her periphery: her mother in a silk wrapper, watching from the window of the front room. Lalita's only there for a minute. She stays until she's sure that Kolia's seen her and then disappears back into the house. She makes them wait outside for another two hours in the end, to teach Kolia a lesson.

The street goes dark blue, then violet; they get cold and shiver. It's summer but cool air drifts over from the Thames. Kolia counts to a hundred – she cries with frustration – she knocks on the door again and again. She grabs handfuls of decorative pebbles from behind the recycling bin and puts them in order from biggest to smallest. Time stretches out into empty spools and she closes her hands on the air as if she can reel it out faster. Every time she hears a passer-by she gets up to look over the hedge, waiting for one of them to be her father on his way back from work.

At last, her mother opens the door. Nino sprints past her and disappears. Lalita smiles like she's played an excellent joke on Kolia, who manages to get all the way to the living room before bursting into tears and throwing herself onto the sofa. There she sits, hot-faced and hugging her knees, blinking furiously at the crystals in the light fixture.

Lalita laughs. 'Did you have an adventure, darling?'

'It's not funny,' she screams. 'You can't leave me outside like that. That's torture.'

Her mother stops laughing immediately. She crosses the room in two steps and slaps her daughter hard across the face. The crystals swing.

'That wasn't torture,' she says. 'You know better than that.'

May 2009

In 2009, the civil war in her mother's birth country is declared over. Her parents get a new Chinese medicine cabinet for the front room. ('The cabinet's antique, actually,' Kolia's father says. 'But it's new to the house.') They buy the cabinet to cover up the message that had been written on the wall in red lipstick. Kolia's mother says she doesn't know why Kolia's father has helped her buy new furniture for a house he so obviously no longer wants to live in. Kolia's father says it's so that when Ammama and Granddad come to stay they aren't immediately confronted with lipstick proof of what a psychotic bitch their daughter is, in case they have double heart attacks and die.

Ammama and Granddad are moving in to No. 25 temporarily. They've been on a world tour of good works ever since her grandfather hung up his stethoscope. They return from each impoverished or war-torn city with souvenir teddy bears and tell Kolia that she needs to look after them extra carefully because they're traumatised. She has a row of bears on her bookshelf now: Freetown, Delhi, Uttar Pradesh. They're coming back now from Palestine. In a month, they'll be off again to teach in rural Malawi but until then they'll stay here. Kolia's grandfather owns No. 25. It's why the master bedroom stays mostly locked up: it's reserved for their visits. Kolia's father unlocks it before they arrive, airs it out. She watches him march round the room, throwing the windows open with too much force, muttering about voluntourism and hereditary delusions of sainthood.

Kolia's grandparents emigrated to England before the civil war. They'd been married when Ammama was only sixteen and moved countries when she was twenty, baby in tow. Ammama likes to tell Kolia that she'd been voted the most beautiful girl in her hometown. Kolia doesn't know Ammama's real name. She knows that she was named after a goddess of marriage, and that this name was then often abbreviated into a shortened form that means queen. But for years now both of these names have been replaced by the epithet 'Ammama', a single designation, a mother's mother. Ammama's very religious. Once she'd bought a white sweater because she'd had a dream where her dead father had given her a white sweater, and afterwards she said the white sweater would work like a protection spell. She has long hair, which she's never cut: a single plait down her back like a seam. When Kolia was a baby, Ammama would let her hair down so that Kolia could brush it until it crackled. She used to tell bedtime stories about rivers of milk and honey, foxes, monkey gods. She used to sing songs in English about rabbits and guns, and in her own language about bees and the moon. She's fanatical about the quality of her English and does the crossword every day. When Ammama had lived in England permanently, before the tour of good works, she seemed to spend all her time playing games. Computer solitaire, computer mah-jong, sudoku, hearts. She'd take long Skype calls with relatives whenever the doctor was out of the house. It won't occur to Kolia until later how very bored Ammama must have been.

The doctor had been a powerhouse before retirement. He'd saved a life at the side of the motorway; he'd been responsible for a serious advance in the understanding of hereditary asthma; he was part of the local Rotary club. He was very politically involved, very socially conscious. He raised huge amounts of money for the people left suffering in his country. (This had so impressed Kolia when she was seven that she stayed up for nights trying to organise her own fund-raiser. She'd only just read the Milly-Molly-Mandy book where Milly turns one penny into five pennies by taking over Miss Muggins's sweet shop and investing in mustard-and-cress seeds and so on, so her vision was a kind of village fête: coconut shies and dogs competing for Best in Show, and all the proceeds going to the war-starved children in her mother's old village. Kolia can remember quite clearly getting as far as the poster and then looking down at it – a pencil drawing of a ribboned dog, on a scrap of lined paper – and being suddenly blinded by clarity that it wouldn't help. It wasn't quite crying over a peacock's corpse but it hadn't been pleasant.) Her grandfather spoke seriously of the devastation that had been experienced by the country's minority population – by their people. That people had a militia, which had been responsible for the initial insurgency, and which had fought the state army for twenty-six years. There were rumours that the doctor sent money to the militia. Kolia overheard her mother make a knowing reference to it. To which he held up one brown finger and replied – do no harm. This made Lalita very angry for some reason. (Kolia only clocked why after she remembered a big fight at Morrisons when her grandfather had thought that the cashier was flirting with Ammama and it had come out during the argument that her grandfather used to beat Ammama, sometimes with a stick. The point was made in English so Kolia could understand.)

*

This time, Kolia gets a Me to You bear from the West Bank with a label that reads *Tatty Teddy*. ('Look,' says her grandfather, pointing at the patch by his ear. 'That's where he was hit by shrapnel.') She tries to play with the West Bank bear, but she's a little too old. She dances him along the windowsills of the master bedroom while her grandparents unpack; Nino snatches him up, dangles him by the ear. 'They should make one of me,' he says.

Trauma is genetic, Kolia's grandfather tells her.

'Oh yeah,' says Kolia. 'I read about this girl who had a phobia of buttons. And no one knew why. And then later she found out that her great-great grandmother or something had actually died choking on a button.' Kolia feels that story very deeply. She can sense, for example, that the button had been red. Her grandfather looks at her like he can't believe how stupid she is.

'Exchange choking on a button with being raped by soldiers and tied to a rubber tyre which is then set on fire.' He has a sonorous voice, heavily accented: a real ship doctor's voice. Then he tells her that she's medically predestined to be an alcoholic. Ammama nods; her mother was.

Mother's mothers, cycling back for ever. Lalita smacks Kolia when Kolia behaves awfully at a party. But this is only because Ammama had smacked Lalita whenever Lalita had bad grades. And this was only because Ammama's mother used to hit Ammama with a stick. And that was only because Ammama was so fair that everyone thought her mother must have had an affair with a colonial officer and so she'd brought shame to her father. But it's more subtle than that too. In fact, Lalita smacks Kolia because her mother had smacked her, and she tells Kolia that she's beautiful because her mother never told her. Ammama smacked Lalita because her mother had hit her and she encouraged Lalita to become a lawyer because her mother had married her off at sixteen. Ammama's mother hit Ammama with a stick because she'd embarrassed her, and she taught her how to fire a gun to fend off the advances of colonial officers.

The blood and the violence of her childhood runs through Lalita in different ways. It turned into the powerful, violent expressions of love that she whispers over Kolia's bed. If some-one is bullying you at school I will turn into a tiger and kill them. If someone touches you and you don't want them to, I will cut his eyes out. And Kolia believes it, because she knows what her mother did for a living. And she feels safe.

Kolia never says 'I'm starving' because her mother told her what starving meant and showed her pictures. She never says 'torture' unless she means it. She'll never complain that her chest is too small, because after the first time she said it Lalita had shown her a photograph of a woman whose breasts had been cut off by soldiers. And at her grandfather's birthday when Kolia was sitting on her Ammama's lap, and they were talking about a woman they grew up with who had been put inside a tyre and the tyre had been set on fire and Kolia started crying and couldn't stop, her grandmother laughed. 'Haven't you ever seen a dead body?' she said.

September 2009

At her new school, Kolia's inundated with worksheets. She draws on all of them so hard she tears the paper. The same drawing every time, compulsively, underneath the date or next to her mark out of ten: a girl bent double, being sick. One hooked line for the figure's arched spine, three twisting lines for the hair falling down over the face, three more a little further down for the vomit, so that the hair and the puke flow into each other like two tiers of the same waterfall. Kolia draws hard enough that if you pass your finger over the paper the waterfall announces itself in negative. She gets sent to a counsellor who is nothing like Mrs Fallada, which is a shame because she's about ready to point at the faceless man digging a hole at the base of the Tree.

Her grandparents still haven't left for Malawi. Ammama packs and repacks the shell suitcases, which stand by the door of the master bedroom under a photograph of a man in orange robes. Granddad has developed a tremor in his left hand. He tells Kolia that the man in orange is a reincarnated saint who had proved his holiness at fourteen by making sweets and flowers appear out of thin air. (He tries to do the trick with a roll of Parma Violets and Kolia sees that the tremor has spread to his right side too.) When Granddad sees the mirror twitch of

Ammama's fingers towards the suitcases, he shouts himself hoarse. He never shouts at Kolia – when she had her spell of nightmares, he sat up with her every night, and made her Ovaltine if she promised to brush again. But he rages at everyone else, fights Kolia's father most of all; wet, croaky bellowing, even after the words have run out.

Ammama camps out in the kitchen, letting Kolia chop and stir under her supervision, one eye on a brutal soap opera, which she doesn't translate. She tells Kolia that the bellowing is also Granddad's illness – that the tremors are a sickness of the brain; the rages are a sickness of the blood. There's a certain madness, a schizophrenic fury that is specific to their people. The babies are born with it.

'Even before the war, I heard so many stories about relatives, about neighbours, who died of anger.'

'Like they had a stroke? Or – just died?' says Kolia, picturing uncles exploding.

'There was a salt that we spread to kill weeds. A chemical salt. We put it everywhere: paddies, potato fields. My brother ate some after our mother told him he couldn't go on the class trip. My friend ate some when her uncle sold their farm.'

On Ammama's phone, the woman in the green sari pushes the man with the carving knife down a well. The fall is shown from seven angles. Kolia thinks she might have it too, this sickness that runs in their blood.

She burns small things in the alley at the side of the house when her father's at work; she melts the blade out of a plastic pencil sharpener. Ammama looks at her knowingly when she comes back in to wash the smell off her fingers. She gets upset about nothing at her new school, steals things from the lab – scalpels and shards of microscope slides, the tiny lily-pad shapes of cross-sectioned aorta disappearing into the silt of her backpack. In the bathroom outside her form room, she pulls her feet up onto the toilet so that no one can tell she's there, but she still gasps with every careful drag of the scalpel, minutely louder every time, to see if anyone takes note.

She's no longer drawing puppies with rosettes. She's graduated, too, from the single long-lashed eye, ubiquitous in the homework diaries of all eleven-year-olds. Now Kolia fills pages with patterns that don't repeat, tendrilled swamps alive with characters – conch, club, lute, skull, skin, bell; arteries and waterlilies; women with ten arms, burned, bangled. Long concentric loops, sinewy and unclosed. The deeply pressed ink is a descendant of the puking girl; the swarming lines a descendant of her puke.

Lalita, still sleeping in the study, tells Kolia she's a genius from down the hall. She buys Kolia acrylic paints and disappears again.

When she comes back, Kolia goes to tuck her in as usual. She kneels next to the mattress where her mother is curled up, brushes out her hair while Ammama gives her a scolding. Lalita's hair doesn't crackle like Ammama's. It falls darkly over the mothy, uncased pillow. Ammama tells her to be a good wife. Lalita can hardly speak. Still, this is the first conversation through which Kolia understands that the end of her parents' marriage is something real and imminent, and not just some horizon with which to one-up Olivia Gadwall's dead dog. A few weeks later, over breakfast, the second conversation begins as an argument about Kolia's school shirt.

Kolia's grandfather considers the importance of an ironed shirt to be on a par with prayer. It's an importance that he impresses not only as a doctor, but as the first brown man to be accepted into Rochdale Rotary club. Yesterday, he was shaking too hard to hold the iron properly, but he refuses to give the job over. There are iron burns on both of Kolia's shirts now.

Granddad vibrates with frustration, his thin shoulders shuddering. The room's filled with the hot smell of ironing spray. Ammama sugars the porridge while Kolia's dad looks for his cufflinks. Kolia's grandfather slams his hands down, and they are frail hands but the whole glass tabletop shakes.

'Where is Lalita?' he roars. 'Where is my daughter?'

The burns on Kolia's shirt are stiff, shaped like the hulls of boats. She tries not to think of the backs burned with irons from the black-and-white photocopies.

'Look around,' yells Kolia's dad. 'Lalita doesn't live here any more.'

Kolia stares. She hadn't been sure.

2014

They hire a boat when her grandfather dies. Kolia's father drops her off at the pier behind the theatre. It's early in the morning; the sky's still dark.

'There's nowhere to park.'

Kolia nods. She's fifteen, has fidgeted the whole ride. Her father squeezes her hand before she gets out, and then he drives off. She keeps her eyes on the car, bruised silver in the dawn, until it makes the right turn where the park begins. Then she turns around.

It's a small, ragtag assembly of mourners that waits behind the theatre. As many as the boat will hold, she guesses. Some are on their phones, some are watching the river. Ammama's smiling straight at Kolia. She's in a maroon velour tracksuit, pottu to match, plumper than she's been in a while. The doctor had died slowly over multiple years and Ammama had taken care of him religiously, totally dutiful, totally disinterested. She wheeled him around, she changed his underwear; when he had to move into the hospice, she continued to spoon-feed him every meal. ('If he could talk, he'd ask us to kill him,' she liked to say, matter-of-factly, before looking back down at the solitaire app.)

After the doctor died, Ammama had invited Lalita to move back into No. 25. Over the past five years, Lalita had lived in fits and starts with the father of Kolia's new baby brothers, but they'd recently, permanently, split. She was happy to return to No. 25; she said she thought the water would be good for her soul. But the whole thing makes Kolia uneasy – resettling a childhood home that she's already left is too much like time-travel, or haunting – and nowadays she spends hardly any nights with her mother.

The boys are gathered at Ammama's side. Archan's fists are fluttering like he wants to run to Kolia, but he knows it's not appropriate. Duly solemn, even at four. The Baby doesn't appear to recognise Kolia. He's sucking his fist, bouncing in the arms of a cousin, a girl Kolia hardly knows but enough of a third-party neutral that Kolia's relieved to see her. Next to the cousin, a man in a puffer jacket leans against a backlit poster for a produc-tion of *A Midsummer Night's Dream*. The donkey mask and pantomime wings glow strangely in the blue early morning. The man looks like he might be related to all of them, though Kolia's fairly sure they've never met. The priest is further off, hands behind his back, peering into the duckweed. He's a perfect priest: round to the point of circular; bare-chested in garlands and an orange sarong with a plait that goes to his waist and ash on his forehead.

Lalita walks up from behind the theatre just as Kolia's wondering about her. She smells of cigarettes. She puts her arm around Archan, whom she'd given her bag to hold, then looks at Kolia like she's just realised she's there.

'Hello, stranger,' she says, and goes to hug her. 'Your hair needs cutting.' At the end of the hug, she smiles tightly down into Kolia's face. 'Perhaps now my father's dead, you'll spend more time at my house.' A rich laugh, to show it's a joke, and a second, one-armed hug. 'Oh, my darling. He loved you very much.'

*

The boat pulls up before she has to respond. It's a cheery river cruiser, painted the off-white of an ice cream van and with a bar below deck. Each mourner is helped aboard by the sprightly, sun-damaged captain, who explains that he's usually hired to ferry tourists to Hampton Court, but he's been booked for this kind of thing too, a couple of times at least. The boat lurches away before Kolia can put her foot on it, an empty sensation, like missing a stair. She gets it right the second time. Before she goes through the little door that will take her below deck, she reads the name printed in blue on the side of the boat: *Meriadoc*.

'*Meriadoc*,' she says to her cousin, hoping to establish the kind of rapport that might see her through the morning. 'Is that from *Lord of the Rings*?'

The cousin shrugs.

The captain herds them below deck, Kolia's stomach still dipping from the way her foot went down onto nothing. She puts Archan on her lap, holds him tightly. The pressure calms her. She hopes it's calming for him too; the boys have been a little edgy since their parents separated. It had been a lurid split, all nosebleeds and shirts cut up and public violence, making the dissolution of Lalita's first marriage look icily sterile. Maybe it's unfair to call the Baby edgy. But over in the cousin's arms, his babbling's turning upset, and he keeps trying to eat the fruit on the offering tray.

The priest ignores him, maintains instead his low, unbreaking chant. He looks out of place on this river-cruiser, whose tables are still sticky with the spilled cider of day-trippers, but Kolia watched him exchange a nod with the captain that identified them as equals. Two men, discharging their ordained duties. She thinks Granddad would have appreciated the priest on the Thames. He'd wanted to go home before he died, but the cease-fire had been so obviously nominal, people still going missing every day. By the time they thought it might be safe, he was already too ill. Archan wriggles. Kolia tries not to stare at the priest's belly button, which goes on for miles.

'We're here,' calls the captain.

The sky is lighter when they go up, clear and quiet. They'd picked this spot more for its water depth and compliance with ash-scattering regulations than out of sentiment, but it's pretty. There's a willow on the bank and an artificial island further down, where small bathing huts have been built. The trunk of the willow has a hairpin bend and the oval leaves trail for metres in the water.

A fleet of six or seven racing kayaks is visible some distance away in the other direction: the Young Mariners' Earlybirds club. They've stopped paddling to observe the boat, and the priest, whose chanting has become louder and more powerful. The teenagers sitting in the kayaks are the very picture of Surrey whiteness. Kolia watches them, braced to hear something racist. She almost wants to hear it. Something in her is spoiling for a fight. By the time the kayakers disperse, Kolia's nearly missed Ammama tipping her husband's ashes into the river.

For a moment the ashes float on the surface like spit. Then the wet pokes through and they go dark, and disappear. Kolia turns to look at her mother, who is smiling rapturously into the water.

2021

The Duck and Rabbit is one of a few riverside restaurants that sit on an expensive stretch of waterfront not far from where Kolia's mother had tried to drown herself. It has red leather booths and a wall of taxidermied rabbits, stuffed whole, mounted like game. Each rabbit is installed lengthways, front and hind legs extended, so that they appear to leap across the plaques. There's neither duck nor rabbit on the menu. Kolia asks for wine; she's twenty-two and has felt older ever since the drowning attempt less than a year ago, but her brothers still gasp at her order. No one else is drinking, even though the dinner is ostensibly a celebration of Ammama's return.

Lalita used to joke that as soon as her father died and Ammama was free, she'd take the inheritance and be off on a tour of the world. They'd be getting photos of Ammama at the Leaning Tower of Pisa and the pyramids. In fact, shortly after the funeral, Ammama went straight back to her hometown to start a school for orphans of the civil war. She hasn't played solitaire since. She's too busy, too fulfilled: glowing with duty. She has power now in the town to which she's returned. She'd left their most beautiful girl and returned one of their richest. After the doctor's death, she expanded. She put on sixty pounds, lost her lower incisors and didn't care – better for sucking mango stones, she says. Now she's the Venus of Willendorf in elasticated slacks. She has let go: she leaks gas, whistles through her teeth. Her hair crackles with power. Her teeth are black at the back and her feet are irreversibly swollen.

Kolia watches Ammama and the rabbits frozen above her. Their glass eyes shine with fear. When Ammama comes back to England – and her visits home are years apart – she carries herself in the way of the self-actualised. (Sheba adores her and obeys her utterly, which irritates Lalita.) She doesn't spend much time with the boys when she's here. Neither of Kolia's brothers had ever got the songs about guns or stories about milk and honey; Ammama doesn't actually seem to like the boys, which, according to Lalita, is due to a general dislike of men. The last time she was over, she'd spent most days ignoring both Kolia's brothers, propping her swollen feet up on Sheba and monitoring the school surveillance cameras from her phone. Occasionally she would burp or fart vigorously, with a completely neutral expression. Her skin shone. Kolia had asked after her routine, having previously heard her grandmother rail against sunscreen. Ammama had smiled with black teeth: 'My skin's so good because I look after God's children.'

The boys have grown since then, though that's not the sort of thing Ammama would comment on. The Baby doesn't even look at the colouring page on the back of the kids' menu. Kolia shuffles up in the booth next to them, thinking that she might avoid conversation with her mother if she's absorbed into the children's end of the table. Her mother's also undergone something of a physical transformation. She likes to say the third pregnancy ruined her body but Kolia thinks it's more the effect of the days her mother doesn't move at all. Her legs and arms are still thin (like matchsticks, says Ammama, putting her fingers around Lalita's wrist) and her fingers are elegant as always. She'd studied classical Indian dance in Hyderabad when she was a girl and it shows in her articulate fingers, gestures that echo the mudras. She's locked in one now, her hands curled out enchantingly, wreathing her chin, framing her face, part Bharatanatyam, part Audrey Hepburn. Unwillingly, Kolia cranes a little out from the children's end to hear what Lalita is saying that demands such an entreating pose.

'Amma,' she hears. 'Can I get the lobster?'

Kolia cringes. Lalita likes to act young whenever she asks her mother for money, which is often. Her extravagant charity and aversion to 'bureaucracy' (admin, emails, final notices) leave her frequently in debt. It baffles Kolia; it galls her: the boys regularly stranded on the other side of London because no one's topped up their Zip cards for months, when Lalita lives rent-free in her mother's house. 'Can I get the lobster?' – a lawyer in her fifties making her voice cute like a child asking for a toy. Kolia cringes, and then the image arrives immediately of her mother eight months ago, teary from the stomach pump. She'd looked like a child for real then, young and dark in the hospital nightgown, craning her neck to see which grown-up had come to collect her, to take care of her, no one in sight but Kolia. The memory flattens out Kolia's wince instantly. Who knows which disdainful eyebrow might be the one to send Lalita over the edge again, which pursed mouth?

She looks happy enough this afternoon, lobster secured. She looks well. She raps a fork against her drinking glass, doesn't stop until the ginger beer fizzes up and every taxidermied rabbit's waiting for the speech to start.

'I want to make sure that you all know how lucky you are, that your Ammama has taken a break from her first love and real family – the school – to come down and be with us all today.' Lalita's delivery's light, humorously bitter, a best man's speech lamenting the end of the party days. It's still a relief when she switches into a show of passionate sincerity. 'No, but I'm so proud of her. She's changing lives. When she started the school, and I really mean started, bricks and mortar, there was nothing like it in the village. Those kids could not read or write. Now the eldest ones are taking English exams. One boy, whose parents were killed by the government's Special Task Force, who still has shrapnel in his head, he's just finished reading *Artemis Fowl*. You loved *Artemis Fowl*, didn't you, Archan?' Archan doesn't reply. He's holding the back of his neck tightly, shielding it from shrapnel. 'And these children aren't just getting an education: they're getting school meals; they're getting care. The work Amma's doing is bigger than you can imagine. She's a saint to these people.' Kolia looks over at her grandmother, pleased by the idea of the old lady saint with the black teeth; Ammama's smiling vaguely at the speech, waiting to go back on her phone. 'I mean a saint. She says she can't stop them from touching her feet – not just the students, their parents, the other teachers. She tries, but they just won't stop. It's a massive responsibility, what she's doing. If I wasn't needed here, I'd be teaching there now. I mean, and also I think there'd be a white van waiting for me as soon as I got out the airport, given the anti-government activities of some of my clients. The point is, there's this thing that runs in our family. It's called Purpose. We help people. And I'm so excited, my darlings, to see what you do with it when it's your turn. For now, let's say thanks,' Lalita lilts back into a cutesy voice, 'to Amma, for coming home, and for our lovely meal.'

Once the speech is done, the food's arrived, Ammama's back to observing live footage of empty classrooms on her phone, Kolia almost relaxes. It feels the climax of the afternoon has passed:

they're on the home run. The boys are organising a game down at the kids' end of the table. The Baby tugs at her sleeve.

'You don't say the word you pick, just how many letters it has. And if you have the most letters, you can go, but you have to be able to spell it,' he explains.

But Lalita's sliding her chair over now, and her gesture is one of delicate interrogation, fingers like a furl of petals. 'Ammama's leaving this weekend, you know, and her room will be free. I thought you might like to move back in for a little bit. Of course, you probably don't want to leave your father all by himself.'

'I don't live with Dad any more, Mum. I have a flat, I told you. And I can't just cut out on my lease. I'm sorry.'

'Archan's going to pick the category,' the Baby's saying. 'But that means he can't have a go, just you and me.'

'Do you want to play?' Kolia asks, tense and upbeat, pressing for levity.

Lalita ignores her. 'Of course, you should see out your lease. I only ask because there's something so depressing about that room going empty again. Just all locked up at the end of the corridor. Like someone's died in it. I know it's my fault. I wasn't there for you when you were younger because I put everything into my work, into helping the less fortunate. And now Amma's doing the same thing, and I'm alone in the house, one room locked up like it's haunted.'

'The category is lizards, but not including dinosaurs.'

'Now we have ten seconds, Kolia. Archan's going to count, okay? Do Mississippi, Archan.'

'You're not alone in the house, Mum. You have the boys.'

'The Baby's at school all day. And Archan locks himself up to play computer games. And they both scream if I try to take it away. Archan's not well, you know. He has terrible anxiety, he takes out it out on me—'

'Two Mississippi, one Mississippi, go.'

'Nine.'

'Oh, um, six.'

'Okay, what's your nine, and can you spell it?'

'—I know it's my fault. I think he would do so much better if you visited, darling. Don't come for me, come for your brother. Both of them, they need you—'

'Cee, aitch, ay, em—'

'—even if I don't deserve it, of course I need you. It helped me so much, you being there, after I did that stupid thing. I don't want to be alone. I need to talk—'

'You can obviously talk to me, Mum. Are you still seeing that woman you found? She was good, I thought.'

'I can't give you this, you're taking too long. Kol, what's your six?'

'Wait! Ee, ell—'

'It's not the same, she can't do anything, really. I'm broke, anyway, and private's the only thing worth doing. But I need you, or . . . I need somebody. And *she* doesn't even listen when she's in the country—'

'Ee, o—'

'Will you SHUT UP, SHUT THE FUCK UP, or I will TAKE YOU TO THE TOILETS and smack you.'

And the Baby stops at once, puts his hands in his lap, quiet as the wall rabbits.

They all go to the airport to see Ammama off. She doesn't come back the next year or the year after, too busy warding the villagers away from her feet. She misses the cleaning fluid incident, the overdose, the roadway catatonia. Each time, as soon as Lalita recovers, she asks where her mother is.

Of course, whenever Ammama gets word of the suicidal gestures, she calls. Over a failing connection on Skype or

FaceTime, she'll remind her daughter to trust in God. If asked to come home, she'll sigh, her skin shining with good deeds. Don't use that voice with her. Doesn't she do enough, letting them stay in that house for free, paying all the household bills that come with it? She's made it clear that when she dies, ownership of No. 25 will pass to the school's trustees; it will be sold and the proceeds donated to the Orphans. Lalita says that she's not worried, because Ammama will outlive them all. The call will lag just before Ammama ends it, screen freezing on a flash of parrot, palm trees mid-rustle, a maid in the background. There's a digital thermostat in the kitchen of No. 25 that sends updates seven thousand miles away, straight to Ammama's phone. If Lalita turns the heating over twenty degrees, her mother turns it right back down. It's ungenerous, verging on unkind. But Lalita puts the heating up in summer sometimes, just to make sure she's still there.

Present

Kolia can't remember the last time she showed up at No. 25 without being invited. She hadn't even called Mia to distract her from the long approach. But she can't acquit Lalita after a single visit, and she'd promised Archan she'd be back. The cleanliness shocks her when she arrives; she'd pictured buzzing flies, overdue post, all the things that are usual when Kolia isn't expected. Instead, Lalita, dazzlingly pleased to see her, leads her down the spotless hallway to the Asian room.

That's what Lalita actually calls it. The Asian room. Really, it's a second sitting room. Kolia hadn't been allowed to play in it when she'd grown up here because it was meant for when guests came over, or clients. Lalita never has guests any more and she takes clients in the front room where she can spread out their histories on the glass table, but the boys still tend to give the Asian room a wide berth. It looks exactly like it sounds. There's a chaise-longue along each wall. One's red damask with little tiger heads carved into the legs; one's been draped in sari fabric and bears a bolster pillow printed with elephants. The red, textured wallpaper is patterned with kalamkari designs; the curtains are shot with gold thread. It's not specifically reminiscent of Lalita's motherland; there's a pan-Asian vagueness to the furnishings. Brass-work, peacocks. Huge candles, with robed men riding elephants coloured into the wax. Incense holders on a low table engraved with dragons. ('Are we dragons?' Kolia had asked. 'I thought we were tigers.' 'We're elephants, darling. Elephants are South Asia, dragons are East. Tigers can be either depending on how the mouth's painted.') There are woodcuts of heavily kohled maharanis and huntresses, Jamini Roy style, and a tapestry of a scene from the *Bahram Nameh* which Kolia finds both compelling and eerie, the painted shahs following you with their wide, sad eyes.

It's funny to think that the room looked basically the same when her dad lived here as it does now, even with strangers having tenanted the house in between. He calls Lalita's style of interior design 'SSLL': Shiny Shiny Look Look. Kolia and her father have a game where they point out items that might be to Lalita's taste: gilded, mirrored things that look like they might fall apart; anything with too much gold leaf on *Antiques Roadshow*. It started when they went to Wales for her cousin's wedding and slept in twin beds in an Airbnb which had a red leather toilet seat that wheezed when you sat on it. Lalita would adore it, they decided, rolling their eyes; she'd hang it on the wall. It was mean of them, Kolia knew. There was a weak valve in her heart that cringed when her mother enjoyed things that were brash, gaudy, loud. She would march straight ahead when Lalita danced to music in the night markets, letting the fruit-sellers spin her. How many of her feelings boiled down to want-ing her mother to minimise herself? How much of that was wanting her to be whiter? The Asian room's part bordello, part stately home antechamber. Kolia thinks the generalised orien-talism of it all sums up Lalita's relationship with her mother-land perfectly: imprecise, deeply and sensually felt, longing rather than knowing. It's Lalita's dirty secret that she hasn't been there in decades, not since before the war.

*

Kolia wonders if it's a bad sign that Lalita's pouring them tea in the Asian room rather than one of her usual nests. She perches on the chaise across from her mother, watching carefully for all the signs: the scratching, the elective deafness, the restlessness. Nothing but the usual obliviousness.

'You have such big bags under your eyes, darling. What have you been up to?'

Kolia pushes her shoulders back. 'Nothing. Teaching. Working on some applications.'

She knows she's made a mistake as soon as she says it. Her mother leans forward eagerly.

'What kind of applications?'

'Just art stuff. Fellowships. Courses. Anything to get out of working, you know.'

Lalita's eyes gleam. 'What do you need? Is it a portfolio thing? Have you been to see the Hiroshige yet? It might be good for inspiration. And Sharon's teaching a course on Russian drawing or something in York at the moment, if you wanted me to give her a call.'

Kolia's stomach aches. A pang in the soft tissue. Part of her responds reflexively to Lalita's zeal, which had been hypnotic when Kolia was little. Lalita would forget to top up her lunch card or have anything in for breakfast or be home to let her in, but she'd commit herself entirely if Kolia gave her the right kind of project. She'd worked for days on a selkie costume for someone's birthday party; she'd written a Petrarchan sonnet in hieroglyphs for a Year 6 papyrus homework. Kolia can feel her eyebrows begin to pull up in a hopeful, canine kind of way, but she forces them straight again, a boot tamping down dirt. She knows this kind of bipolar parenting too well, how it ensnares, how it stretches to breaking point and then collapses. Neoprene and twisted flax are bad substitutes for consistency. Anyway, the applications are mostly random – a handful of programmes from Marseille to Maastricht, a gesture towards thinking about the future. She changes the subject.

Lalita lists recent victories in her ongoing dispute with the Bar Standards Board, breaking off every so often to gaze at Kolia lovingly. She looks well, as well she ever does. These days, she keeps odd hours. She does her paperwork after dinner and into the middle of the night. She operates strangely: she doesn't have any of what Kolia's puritanical father calls 'work hygiene'; she'll organise papers on any surface, surrounded by food, a show on another screen; she'll doze off in between detailing the detention centre mistreatment of her clients. But by all accounts her work is still exceptionally good.

Nevertheless, she's doubled in size since the first time she lived in No. 25. She keeps her nails short now: over the course of various manic episodes, she has scratched deep scars into the skin on her face and arms. Her breathing rasps; her hair is falling out at the temples. Her time is taken up with paperwork or remote hearings. She smells of cigarettes and sour wool, and rarely leaves the house. Perhaps Kolia's assessment of her mother is sexist. It definitely feels like a product of automatic, involuntary distaste, rather than reason. Sometimes, when Lalita is scratching long rills into the side of her dry neck, Kolia feels her lip curl reflexively, and Lalita says, 'You look just like your father right now.'

Lalita thinks that being raised chiefly by her father was bad for Kolia's politics. ('But you were already a little Tory,' she says, when she's very angry. 'Or you wouldn't be picking the white male parent.') It's true that the dynamic has coloured Kolia's instincts. The Shiny Shiny Look Look game is proof of that. She doesn't really think she's been somehow infected with mis- ogyny; it's more that she was raised in an exception to the rule of motherly sacrifice, and generally male abusers, and 'Believe Women'. Lalita was always more like the vintage, traditional father, that remote outpost of freedom, carelessness, self-indulgence: Jack Kerouac, going out to get cigarettes and never coming back. Which is to say, if either of Kolia's parents were to have a secret second family, it would be Lalita, without a shadow of a doubt.

Lalita's interrupted by the scrabbling sound of Sheba hurtling down the mopped corridor to greet the boys at the door, and then the sound of the boys throwing themselves on Sheba. She smiles at the noise: a true smile that makes Kolia's heart squeeze painfully. The boys pile into the Asian room.

'Kolia, I knew you were here, I saw your shoes.'

'Mum likes working in here now but we're not allowed to sit on the sofa.'

'We can sit on the sofa if we're doing our homework, I think.'

A compromise is reached, where Archan can sit on the chaise if he takes his blazer off first and the Baby can sit on Kolia's lap, because that's not sitting on the chaise, not technically. They're undisguisedly excited to see her; she can tell they weren't expecting her back so soon. That's the reason she's there, really. Ammama, seen off at the airport, gone for too long.

'Do you remember that game,' Kolia asks them. 'The one with the categories?'

'Is it called Categories?'

'The one where you have to think of the longest word.'

'Yes, I know it, it's called something else. Can we play it?'

'Are you staying tonight?'

Kolia looks at Lalita, who's pretending not to have heard Archan ask. 'Yeah, I think so. If that's okay.'

*

All the doors in the house have real locks, real keys. Solid doors with iron handles and iron latches. The keys are intricate, with twisting designs in the bows: labyrinths of leaves and flowers, teardrops and faces. Kolia has the only spare key to the master bedroom. Mantilla scrollwork, hiding hook, eye, heart, wheel – sigils, to her child's eye, for everything that waited unknown on the other side of the door. It's been nearly a year since she last spent the night, but whenever she does, she stays in Ammama's room. It's Kolia, now, for whom the room awaits; Kolia upon whose rare visits the house turns.

The master bedroom has its own microclimate as a result of lying undisturbed for months at a time. It's warm, airless. The framed photos of gods and gurus keep company with a type of odd beige insect that Kolia's only ever seen in this room. They're some kind of housefly, unusually light-coloured, but she always thinks of them as silverfish because the name sounds right. The sheets are clean and stale and there's a huge, low butler's desk, made of the same dark wood as the colonial sofa and the medicine cabinet downstairs, but covered in clotted dust. Tonight, she goes through the drawers. Inside are photo albums, a substantial collection of hotel matchboxes, and folders of information about Lalita, all shut away. Kolia opens the folders, which contain documents underscoring Ammama's responsibility for her daughter: psychiatrist reports, signed releases from various institutions. She begins to read through one and finds that she can't finish it.

PART 3: THE WHITEST BROWN PERSON YOU KNOW

1.

At the beginning of *Around the World in Eighty Days* is a passage in which Jean Passepartout, valet and secondary protagonist, describes his new employer.

> Phileas Fogg was, indeed, exactitude personified, and this was betrayed even in the expression of his very hands and feet; for in men, as well as in animals, the limbs themselves are expressive of the passions.
>
> He was so exact that he was never in a hurry, was always ready, and was economical alike of his steps and his motions. He never took one step too many, and always went to his destination by the shortest cut; he made no superfluous gestures, and was never seen to be moved or agitated. He was the most deliberate person in the world, yet always reached his destination at the exact moment.
>
> He lived alone, and, so to speak, outside of every social relation; and as he knew that in this world account must be taken of friction, and that friction retards, he never rubbed against anybody.

Kolia's father gave her a copy of *Around the World* for her ninth birthday. She recognised him in this passage immediately, and, between the gifting and the description, she's associated her father with Fogg ever since. He's a man of straight lines and right angles; not like Enzo's mother (flashing, Vorticist), but like a set table. He likes abstract, geometric paintings and when she was a teenager, he had her posters framed, all the slouchy American singers surrounded by crisp white mounts. For forty years, he's diarised his appointments in the same journal, a graduation gift from his mother. Age has flattened the binder leather into a textureless rectangle: an object from a pristine, one-dimensional world.

His professorship is in mathematics, specifically the study of computer-aided medical procedures. Nevertheless, with arithmetical precision, he learns about the artists that Kolia's studying so that he can send her relevant links: back issues of copier zines, exhibitions to catch. He calls to check that she's got to the other end of a long train journey. He gets squeamish about knitting needles and forks in the toaster, all the disasters that might befall his daughter. And, not having the sense of guardian angels that Lalita does, he guards against those disasters prosaically.

Her father is solitary – not as housebound as Lalita, but inflexible in his habits. Kolia had once come across a factoid from a family therapist, claiming that everyone needed four hugs a day for survival, eight hugs a day for maintenance, and twelve hugs a day for growth. Horrified by this, she personally aims for four, and when she's home, tries to dole them out to her father, not being able to picture him hugging anyone at work in his stiff suit. When she was little, she would hug him in the evenings and smell the kitchen on his clothes. She felt bad for him then, embarrassed for him. But now she can recognise the smell for what it was: simply one of the less adorable hallmarks of adulthood. In those days she hadn't been clued in to the chopping of parsley; Lalita, of course, only ever wore Jo

Malone. By breakfast, her father smelled of cologne and coffee again. He would play Radio 4 from his laptop while he got ready for work and blink consideringly at whichever bishop was reading 'Thought for the Day'.

These remembered mornings don't take place at No. 25 but in the house where Kolia and her father had lived afterwards. They'd moved almost down the road. Same town, different furniture; an antique nautical clock still sits on his desk, which rings in confusing increases every half hour until it hits eight bells. Her father still lives here; he sleeps in a single bed that had been Kolia's when she was tiny. He'd bought her a new one for the new home, and only meant to store the old twin-size in his room for the transition period. But, in a case of uncharacteristic inertia, or perhaps more characteristic frugality, he still hasn't replaced it more than a decade later. Kolia takes pictures sometimes when she catches him napping in her old bed. He goes pink when he sleeps; his face seems soft and bare without his glasses and his closed eyes draw attention to the skin exposed where his eyebrows are thinning (he rubs them while he's thinking). He looks younger, defenceless.

Today her dad's routine is similar to the routine he had when Kolia was at school. He exercises three times a week, runs down by the pale river, records it on an exercise watch. (He has two watches, plus the ship's clock: one's a rubbery own-brand Fitbit; the other's a proper Phileas Fogg watch, which he saves for special occasions.) At the weekends, he cycles long distances on an electric mountain bike. There's a thin scar down his side from an off-road bike race in the Pindus mountains. Sometimes Kolia wonders if her mother was misled by the scar into thinking that her father was dangerous and exciting. This is partly a constituent of her broader wondering about how they could

ever have ended up together, and partly because Lalita once
dated a guy with two AK-47s tattooed on his chest.

Her father hasn't seen Lalita in years, though they live twenty
minutes from each other. When Kolia was much younger and
they were still sharing custody, her father would ferry her
between the houses. Every time he dropped her off, the boys
would appear curiously at the door. 'They're fascinated by my
glasses,' her father explained, and he'd take them off for the
boys to play with. He refuses to see them now, even if Kolia's
staying at his and just wants to have them over for dinner. He
doesn't want to get to know them, in case the next time he
hears about Lalita doing something obviously negligent he feels
that he has to get involved.

Fair enough to decide that co-parenting with Lalita once is
the limit. Even Kolia's teachers had commented on the chasm
between their child-rearing. Her father wrote absence notes
with a fountain pen, on letter paper with lined paper underneath to keep his handwriting level. Her mother had once sent
her to school with a note excusing her for having forgotten her
PE kit which, when Kolia opened it, just said, 'We are divorced.'
It became a go-to saying at her father's house, whenever excuses
were needed, just – 'we are divorced'. Funny sort of like the
Ammamamama joke, which is to say not funny at all.

The Ammamamama joke always reminds Kolia of just how
English her father is. He's so English he'd been a Boy Scout.
This was anathema to Lalita, who maintains that Scout troops
are feeding schools for the armed forces, but in practice only
means that he keeps a little red pouch of first aid supplies in the
bathroom cabinet, from which he used to take a pair of twee-
zers whenever Kolia got a splinter.

Their town – the towpaths, bandstands, lawns and tennis
courts of it all – suits him down to the ground. When it is icy in

the park and Kolia has to hold her father's arm and the Stepford houses on the other side of the river shine, she can't picture him anywhere else. He has a Historic Royal Palaces membership card and they used to cycle up to Hampton Court Palace quite regularly. They could follow the Thames straight from their house to the palace, which made Kolia feel like part of a previous century. Once they'd stopped their bikes on the grassy bank for a white moaning shape which had turned out to be a swan, or two swans: a mother and her dead cygnet. The noises the swan made had been as similar to crying as a bird can get, and when Kolia had looked up, her dad was using his thumb to wipe a tear from his serious, bald eyes. She remembers it with a painful warmth.

Mostly they got to the palace without stopping, so that he could stroll through the stone hallways with his hands clasped behind his back and she could read in the wooden window seats that looked down on the maze. Kolia doubts it was his intention, but the effect was a childhood sense of old England that was beguiling, strong and firm compared to her impressionistic sense of her mother's other, island country. She never articulated this to Lalita, who would have hated it. God, maybe being raised by the white man *was* bad for her politics.

Her father has never been to the country of Lalita's family. In the last few years he's been travelling a lot for work – Strasbourg, Heidelberg, occasionally Johns Hopkins. He's in Munich at the moment, conferring on a new method of imaging skin lesions. Kolia only recently realised that these invitations hadn't started coming out of nowhere: he'd been turning them down for eighteen years beforehand. It's still strange to her that he goes to all these hotels, expensed by far-flung conferences, and then comes home to a rickety twin-size bed, but she supposes inertia has a different kind of pull at home. Or, more generously, that he's reached a kind of post-divorce equilibrium and is resistant to change.

She knows that her father hopes that one day she'll enjoy the same equilibrium. It's why he supports all of her token applications to art programmes. It's why he looks so disappointed whenever Lalita lures Kolia back onto speaking terms. He can't exactly tell Kolia to ignore her mother's distress signals, but his advice is the same every time.

Don't let her suck you back in. Don't let her put your life on hold.

2.

Kolia wakes up with the same peculiar feeling that comes over her when she spends the night at Gabriel's or on Mia's sofa, especially if she's slept badly or been drinking: a feeling that she's woken up in her childhood home, that she's sixteen years old, that the last ten years were all a dream. It takes longer than usual to shake. Another dazed minute before she remembers that it's true, partly – she'd slept over in the master bedroom. She turns over in her grandparents' old bed and startles. Lalita is right there, leaning in the open doorway, staring at her.

It's not clear how long she's been there but her fixed, blissful expression doesn't drop when Kolia sees her. She's smiling, almost shyly, radiating her thoughts with humble transparency: delight at her daughter's presence, pleasure in watching her sleep, a kind of pride in her having stayed the night for the first time in years. Kolia assumes this is what Glenn Close looks like in *Fatal Attraction*, just before she boils the bunny.

She pulls the covers up to her chin. 'Do you mind? I have to get ready for work.'

Devna has a new spoon for disembowelling the pomegranates, with a serrated edge. She stands at the counter without moving for half an hour. Kolia thinks she might be detaching the seeds from their sockets one by one. She works and watches, judgemental like a statue, with a braid that comes down to her sweatpants.

Her hair is longer than Kolia's, and darker.

Once, when Kolia had just started, Devna had asked her if she could speak Hindi. She'd looked betrayed rather than disappointed by the answer. It's since been made it clear that there's no room for camaraderie; she's devoted to Francesca and, Kolia suspects, has reported her at least once for stealing fruit roll-ups from the snack drawer.

Focusing feels hard today, even without Enzo screaming. The logic questions seem to have devolved.

Assume that some scuts are vuks, all tox are carx, and some pites are scuts.
Therefore it makes sense that:
A: some vuks may also be pites
B: all scuts are vuks
C: all tox are pites
D: some carx are vuks
E: all tox are scuts

Kolia misses the pings and lings. The question setter for this paper seems to have chosen these sinister, angry sibilants and fricatives on purpose. Tox and carx and scuts are cruel sounds, possibly curse words; vuks and pites sound like slurs. Enzo sounds especially like a horror-movie child today, reading the question out in his little sing-song.

She looks up at his drawings, hanging all around her. This morning they radiate the spacing and madness and crayon-texture of children's drawings in horror films. Enzo makes a lot of sense as the little boy behind those. You know the one: he draws his 'new friend from school' only for it to be a man with knives for hands. He draws the dream he had the other night and it's the house on fire with a face in the window. He's been drawing in the corner of the room all movie and when the mum finally looks it's just the word 'death' over and over.

Tiny, spoiled prince of darkness. My brothers would eat you up, thinks Kolia.

She tears her eyes away from the dog's fifth crosshatched leg when Enzo's mother comes in, and says 'So, all tox are carx.'

Francesca doesn't seem to care whether or not Kolia acts like she's teaching. She sweeps over to her son with the plate of pomegranates from the counter and sets them in front of him, like it's her work, like she's shelled those jewels. Enzo eats them with a fork and his mouth turns red.

'How are you, Kolia?' says Francesca, sweetly. 'How are your family?'

'They're great.' Kolia smiles.

She tries never to deviate from this response, because once she had to cancel a lesson to pick Lalita up from the hospital where they were examining her for hypoxia, and Francesca's asked about Lalita's health ever since, intermittently but with a deeply irritating concern, as though she were somehow deficient, as though Francesca would never dream of being at risk for hypoxia. If Kolia does talk about her mother, she'll mention that she's busy with a new case or that she's taken on a new pupil. Partly, this is to reaffirm Kolia's own pedigree – professional parents and a grammar-school upbringing – which she knows is what's got her in the door of this big, steel kitchen. But it's also, unavoidably, a secret dig at Francesca's idle, non-life-saving existence.

This one's a misogynistic tendency that Kolia's definitely absorbed from her mother rather than her father: instinctive disdain for the stay-at-home mother. (The *rich* stay-at-home mother, she'll clarify, desperately.) The rich stay-at-home father isn't any better, Mia tells her. Mia's boss, the melty blonde, does something very high powered for an airline company, and Theo's father just slinks around the house while Mia teaches, looking vaguely dispossessed in his T-shirt and boxers.

When Mia talks about Theo's career-woman mother and her browbeating abilities with obvious relish, Kolia comes back, pettily, to the time that she'd told Mia a story about one of her old childminders, a Scottish woman whose hair changed colour every week, and Mia had laughed. 'One of? God, it makes so much sense that you were raised by a series of nannies.' She wasn't saying it with malice but for a moment Kolia had been flooded with defensive, disproportionate rage, fourteen again, setting little fires in the alley at the side of the house. 'Because both my parents worked!' she'd replied hotly and only just refrained from making a jab at Mia's mother, whose job, when she felt like it, was advising other women on what furniture to buy for their failing boutiques.

Sometimes Kolia thinks the real truth of her character is this fractiousness that only Mia brings out. It's not about the nannies; with Mia, and really only Mia, she'll take exception to a dish put away wet or a book left butterflied.

The roots of the fractiousness are threefold. It's partly that Kolia's so used to being on the lookout for fault with her mother that her default mode is correction. Her father's the same way: to put it generously, precise. In her weakest state, small things – leaving teabags in the sink in the summertime – are direct affronts. Perhaps because these little slip-ups so often distinguished Kolia's mother's house from her father's, they'd blurred into the more heinous negligence. (When Kolia was a kid, she'd liked oranges the most, a liking born out of Lalita's house, where meat was left out and milk spoilt. There was no telling how long food left on the counter had been there nor what it had been in contact with, and so she took great comfort from oranges, clementines, tangerines, whatever appeared on whichever soiled surface, sealed from contagion in their rinds.)

The fractiousness is also a result of closeness. Kolia would never say, *Francesca, don't hand me your bag like that; Enzo, don't take food off my plate; Gabriel, wash your hands before you play with my hair*, so she saves it all for Mia.

And, of course, there are aspects of Mia that are simply difficult. Beautiful, spoon-fed so much love that she still makes her hands open and shut like crab pincers when she wants you to pass her the salt. These things are obviously irritating, but the thing in Kolia that rises to them would exist in their absence. It exists always, this fractious child, oversensitive to everything, tightness in its shoulders, grit in its clothes; it just rarely thumps the table.

'I could never do what your mother does,' says Francesca, in a way that suggests she's very at peace with that.

Kolia forces her shoulders down, wrings out a smile. She shakes her head, like, *Don't be ridiculous.* 'Being a mum is a full-time job!'

Enzo fusses away from his mother. Behind the counter, Devna's still working the silent, serrated spoon. It's someone's full-time job at least.

3.

She eats dinner in Mia's mother's perfectly furnished kitchen that evening. Both Mia's parents are out of town and their place in Shoreditch has been taken over: spillages on a long table, cutlery and jewellery glittering in the lamplight. It's late; everyone's already drunk and outlandish from hunger. It doesn't feel like they're in a family home. Maybe that's the fourteen hand-picked dining chairs, all amputations from larger sets, all subtly different shades of lavender and clay. Maybe it's just the tenor of the evening, or the associations Kolia makes with Hoxton: wild nights out, being sick in the street.

She's sitting across from Gabriel, who's wearing one silver earring and keeps forgetting that they can't smoke inside. He hasn't mentioned the call she'd made from the third floor of the shopping centre, which she supposes is a good thing. He asks ironic questions about her job instead and they all laugh about the little child who loves to scream.

She tops up her glass and turns around, where she spots a photo of Mia easily, and another and another. Mia has two brothers, meaning multiple-aperture picture frames.

'These are so fucked,' says Kolia, pointing them out, tri-cut mounts in cream cardstock. 'They always put the favourite child in the middle.'

'It's oldest to youngest, you psycho,' says Mia, looking pleased. She's always in the middle.

Perhaps it's to her disadvantage, this favouritism. Mia's brothers are now famously high-achievers; meanwhile, she's stuck tutoring the peacock-killer, wondering why something feels like it's missing. The photo sings in its frame: Mia, tucked between the oncologist and the coastal engineer, pretty and love-fed and unprepared for wanting.

Kolia thinks about Enzo's drawings and how his mum proves she cherishes them by surrounding them with unnecessary white space. Maybe you could do it with words too; maybe you need lots of silence around your sentence for it to stand out. She doesn't know half the people here. Gabriel and Mia are points of starlike clarity on which she fixes her conversation.

Enzo's an easy punchline, like Lalita. Sometimes Kolia gives out her mother's Valium like favours. Sometimes she tells stories where Lalita's raging saviour complex is the butt of the joke, although Mia often objects to these. (*I think it's gorgeous your mum's got all this purpose. Genuine holy telos. Isn't that what we're all looking for? Like, I wish I had some holy telos.*) Tonight Kolia's recounting the time that Lalita went into H&M and asked if she could get a discount because she was a human rights lawyer. The anecdote's a joke but it had nevertheless been one of Kolia's most embarrassing experiences, and so she still has to suppress a feeling of betrayal when Mia replies with 'Right. And if the world was fair, she'd get one. What are you, team H&M?'

'I know,' Kolia says, 'God. She's always said the best way to rebel against her would be to become a conservative, and I'm at the top of the slippery slope.'

'Yeah.' Another girl laughs. She's blonde and pretty; Kolia knows her from parties, forgets her name. 'You're like the whitest brown person I know.'

*

Shutting the bathroom door behind her feels like coming up for air. These nights always go one of two ways, and this one's going the way that makes Kolia feel hopeless. These dinners would happen for ever and Gabriel would never kiss her stomach again. These dinners would happen for ever and she can imagine everything they would ever say.

'You should try CBT.'

'I really want to travel.'

'I would never want to have kids anywhere other than London—'

'Did you know Ottolenghi delivers?'

'—which means I need to get the living abroad done *now*.'

'It's actually just a lip-gloss and some tint.'

'I wish people would stop saying that cider's a femme drink.'

'She's really not a coffee person.'

'—but once you have a child, everything's new—'

'You should try CBD.'

'There's nothing better than being your own boss.'

'—you just become a tourist in your own town.'

'Did you know Nobu delivers?'

She looks in the mirror and tops up her lip-tint with a gloss. It would all be quite nice if she could do it with someone she liked. Or maybe Mia's right, and she really just needs some holy telos to take the edge off. When Kolia puts the make-up back in her bag's zip pocket, she finds the little brown bottle of Vyvanse, which she strokes consideringly. Her phone lights up suddenly in her bag. The lining of her bag flashes in response, with appropriate franticness. The messages are bad.

Kolia returns to the table but doesn't sit down. She puts a hand on the back of her chair. 'I think I have to go, you guys.'

'Oh no!'

'What's up?'

'Is it your mum?' says Mia, who loves showing that she knows about people's problems.

The fractious child in Kolia rolls her eyes, but she just nods. 'Yeah. Honestly, I think it's insensitive to quote anyone under the age of thirteen, but Archan sounded quite scared.'

Some murmurs; some discussion of being thirteen.

Gabriel reaches out over the food towards her arm. 'Please stay; I haven't seen you in ages.'

Kolia hopes she doesn't look ecstatic.

She knows she's needy when it comes to relationships – intensely, sometimes pathologically. She has a system for controlling it – she's identified this, her one craziness, and she has a mnemonic to alert her so she can stop it in its tracks. The mnemonic is SCOPP, which stands for: Seeking Care ('*I've had a really hard day*'); Over-analysis (reading too much into phrasing, and punctuation); People-pleasing (self-explanatory); Preoccupation with appearance (viewing her looks as either the root of the problem or its solution, leading either way to maniacally focused beauty regimes and self-depilation.) Now, Archan's texts bright in her bag, Kolia runs through SCOPP to see if she's making the needy choice, the crazy choice. But this isn't a SCOPP scenario. Gabriel's begging her to stay; she's cutting herself some slack. Sometimes she reassures herself that if Lalita got two men to marry her, Kolia can't possibly be that hard to love.

Gabriel talks about his problems on the way back to his house. Kolia slips her hand in his, her best comforter-child move, the way she used to walk next to her mother as a kid, back when she was Lalita's favourite sounding board.

It's awful how much pleasure Kolia can take in very mediocre sex. Phatic fucking: minimally effective stimulation but when

Gabriel talks about what he wants from her body, what he's happy to imagine it can give him, she's floating. It doesn't reflect on the sex itself that she leaves her body a little. Kolia thinks all girls do it. When she hovers out she can appreciate for a moment that his arm goes all the way around her waist, but before she knows it she's looking at the square dining table in the otherwise empty room next door. She's been dragged past all the bare walls, loo rolls pitifully stacked on top of the cistern, and is opening the fridge – six Kronenbourgs roll about in the bright light like wounded soldiers – before she manages to centre herself back in their two bodies.

Gabriel hands her a towel. It's raining outside. His flat is right at the top of a fairly empty new build and she can hear the rain better from higher up. The smell of hot pavement rises and she misses, suddenly, deeply, a story she used to read when she was a kid, the first story that taught her that everyone likes the smell of cut grass.

Kolia likes the idea of the two of them alone together, far above the ground. It feels good, if fragile. She's not a perfectionist when it comes to homemaking, but the bareness of Gabriel's walls makes it seem like he's always on the cusp of moving in or out. In fact, he's been here for six months without putting up a poster, or curtains, or ever appearing to have stocked his fridge. The only decorative thing in the entire flat is a sculpture by Gabriel's mother, a well-known ceramicist. Kolia has never met Gabriel's mother, but according to the internet she specialises in collages of organic forms. Disembodied limbs, bones, driftwood. The piece on Gabriel's bedside table is a mosaic of sand and stone, in a bolted-bronze frame shaped like a porthole. Kolia cut her hand once, trying to pick it up. On closer inspection, she could see that there were little bits of broken glass sticking up out of the mosaic.

She gets back into Gabriel's bed, eye-level with the spiky little disc.

Gabriel turns onto his side towards her.

'Okay, weird thought. Weird, sexual thought.'

'Obviously go on.' Kolia presses her face into his shoulder.

'Okay. When your tits were in my mouth. I wished – momentarily – there was milk coming out. Is that weird? Momentarily!'

(Kolia has never met Gabriel's mother, but she does think of her now.)

She feels for a second that it should have been a little less easy for him to confess. 'It's not weird. It's not my cup of tea, I think.' She intertwines one of her legs with his to show that she's not totally revulsed.

After Gabriel falls asleep, Kolia scrolls through the Wikipedia page for erotic lactation. The first thing that surprises her is how common it appears to be. The next is that it's especially common in lesbian relationships, which Kolia finds comforting. It might be irrational, but she feels like the sexual psyche of a woman who's attracted to women is probably less addled with harmful things than the sexual psyche of a straight man. She's less comforted by a story at the bottom of the page, *Caritas Romana*, about the exemplary virtue of a Roman woman who breastfeeds her starving father. A version of the same story crops up at the end of *The Grapes of Wrath*, which is a book that Gabriel calls his favourite despite only having read half of it. It's been a regular joke of theirs – how like a man to love a book he hasn't finished. What a lucky coincidence. She gets up to pee in the middle of the night, and afterwards stares at her face in the mirrored doors of Gabriel's bathroom cabinet for so long that the reflection begins to swim. She's breaking out on her forehead. She opens the doors, splitting her face in half.

In the morning, in the small window where she's awake and he's asleep, everything that might be second-guessed falls away. She delights in what's left: the sunlight on his shoulder, the small movements of his throat, the undreaming eyelids. She studies his chest as it rises and sinks, the abrupt boundaries of the hair there.

A fractional shift in his breathing, and she's immediately aware that she's slipped into the *Fatal Attraction* gaze. And now she can feel the texts from her brother burning a hole in the bedside table. Kolia straightens her eyebrows, tamps down the need in her face, a boot on loose dirt again.

She rolls out from under the duvet and lets herself out before Gabriel wakes up. It's good practice anyway, leaving before you're told to go.

4.

She's nearly at No. 25 before she knows it, the long, hot road disappearing beneath her, the shrubs shrinking away. Sometimes it's as if Lalita's hiding behind these hedges, like some post-celebrity with too much surgery who never opens her curtains. For the first time, it occurs to Kolia, who can still feel recent sex in her thighs and her sit-bones, that her mother might be unhappy about her body. She's never considered that a possibility, probably because Lalita carries herself, however slowly, with such pride and self-assurance. She always has. She's never denigrated her appearance, which contributed immensely to Kolia's own sense of being safely gorgeous when she was younger. It was one of the best things she'd done as a mother. Even after she put the weight on, she'd look in the mirror and go: *God, I think I have reverse body dysmorphia. Or, God, it's difficult being the most beautiful woman in the world.* It was in the same voice that she pronounced her daughter flawless, or called all her drawings masterpieces. (For a while, believing her, Kolia grew up thinking that she was an artist of rare talent.)

The declarations didn't stop even after Kolia had begun to question her mother's judgement. Even after the morning, a wet morning, in summer, just before Kolia moved into her dad's house for good. A wet morning, rain rattling the garden doors, a smacked face, a broken bowl; 'I didn't realise it was possible to hate your own daughter.' The rain had stopped in the afternoon, Kolia had been painting, a scrawling, slapdash painting, a revenge painting, like nothing so much as the message in lipstick behind the cabinet in the front room, a painting that called her mother a cunt, a freak, evil in red oils, until a murmur had her turning around. Lalita was leaning against the door frame, admiring the painting the same way you'd admire a child's perfect sandcastle. 'Fantastic,' she'd said seriously. 'Genius.'

Of course, once she'd understood that her mother could be capable of real, certifiable delusion, the power of her compliments slipped away. Kolia started looking at her drawings more critically. By the time Lalita had been saved by the guardian angel of the cycle path, Kolia was finding fault with every stray line or misjudged cross-hatching. Later on, she found a kind of peace in printmaking, its soothingly identical copies. There's no chance of error once the master plate is perfected, and there's the added satisfaction of peeling out the negative space, making bone-deep grooves in soft tile; the pleasure of differently shaped scalpels.

(Sometimes, still, dancing in Hoxton, she feels ineffably beautiful – the most beautiful woman in the world! She hears it in her mother's voice. She feels silly afterwards.)

Now, ringing the bell, Kolia looks at her reflection in the stained-glass panels of the door. The brown package tape, which holds one of the panels in place, wraps around and through her reflected face. This is a well-framed portrait. This is the aperture she deserves.

Lalita opens the door, ecstatic when she realises who it is. 'I wasn't expecting you! Do you want some balm? Your lips are looking very dry, sweetheart.'

Kolia presses them together, wondering if they had been dry that morning when she'd left Gabriel's. 'No, thanks. Where are the boys?'

'They're at their dad's.'

'Oh.' Kolia goes in anyway. It's probably better that they're not here while she's canvassing the house for evidence of mistreatment. The lens engages as soon as she's in the hallway and it sets her off-kilter. She's no longer a woman who's recently slept with the guy she likes and who told him very casually to text her whenever; she's not even a girl, just something angry and small, trying to make sense of her mother's actions.

It's been a long time since Kolia grew up here. When she lived in No. 25, Lalita was still married to her father. Past violences loom up at her as she walks the halls, looking for proof of new misdemeanours. The covered-up lipstick message blares from the room downstairs, like an alarm on a ghost frequency. She's going slowly, not frantically. A detective who doesn't want the murderer to know he's been clocked. Lalita follows her around, smiling. 'I'll make you a tea', she says. She doesn't move. Kolia looks for broken crockery, torn documents, anything that bears witness to the fit Archan had described. But she can only see – that bed, where Lalita pushed her off and she cracked her skull – that doorway, where Lalita pulled her, Solomon style, out of her father's arms and screamed. The walls are almost the same. New stains, a new photo, these estrange her, make them slide out of focus. The stair-carpet is different from the one Kolia grew up with but the banisters are the same. If she investigates the house like this, looks closely, the whole thing's out of sync. It's another world. Another cycle. That is not the bedroom she had turned five, six, seven in. That is not the bathtub she had shared with her mother when she was too young to float.

What does Lalita see? Sometimes Kolia thinks the island haunts the house. The house belongs to the island, after all. By way of the Orphans.

Lalita doesn't look haunted. 'What are you looking for, darling?'

'I wanted to see if everything was okay. The boys sounded really frightened last night.'

'Oh, you should have said. God, of course. What, did they text you that I was getting angry – that I was being crazy?' Lalita laughs. They're lying, she explains. Kids lie. The fact is that Archan had an outburst when she'd threatened to take away his gaming set-up. It was a frightening outburst, too, swearing, screaming. She says that she'd thought he might hit her.

'So I told him I was going to tell you, and that you'd be very disappointed in him. It worked as if I was saying that I had Santa on the phone. They absolutely worship you, you know. He'll have said anything to cover his back, bless him. They just want you round here more, darling.'

'He said you threw stuff at him. He said you broke his favourite cup.'

Lalita shakes her head. 'Kids lie,' she says again. 'Don't start making a conspiracy out of it this time.'

Kolia's honestly not sure who to believe: her baffling adult mother or two children. Kids do lie. Kolia was lying almost constantly at that age. But Lalita lies too. Once, after threatening to overdose, she'd sent Kolia a series of nonsense, garbled texts that seemed to confirm that she was insensible, slipping off into unconsciousness; later, Kolia learned that she'd been texting her solicitor completely lucidly at the same time, perfect spelling and everything. Kolia thinks of her mother's gallstones, in quotes, as her dad puts them. She thinks of her father saying 'Don't let her suck you back in!'

Lalita often suggests that Kolia stopped living with her as a result of Lalita being a working mother, unable to put a whole roast dinner on the table every night. But Kolia had stopped living with her because there were often smashed plates. Or clothes being cut up, or wrists grabbed and pulled. The nights when no one was at home were better than the nights Lalita wished she was dead. Something sudden would set her off. She would see in it evidence that her daughter didn't love her, or had betrayed her, or was laughing at her. She would nurse the evidence until it became truth and then she would break.

Sometimes Kolia wants to smash plates too. She has actually thrown a cup. She'd thrown it a metre wide of her first boyfriend, who had hated the mollifying tone that Kolia adopted in moments of conflict. 'You don't have to pretend everything's okay,' he'd told her, not in a sympathetic way, but in a withering, patronising way. Like he thought the idea of rage hadn't even occurred to her. He wanted her to throw it, really.

(Embarrassing, the way it's always love that makes Kolia feel most like her mother. SCOPP, SCOPP, SCOPP. When she's crying on the bathroom floor, doing iMessage-response-time maths, holding her head in her hands, wanting to hold his. The days where her romantic feelings come in moderation feel like days of sudden clarity, perfect relief.)

Lalita takes her through to the kitchen and stands in front of the cabinet with her hands on her hips. 'Look,' she says. 'Anything missing?'

Kolia tries not to think about the text she'll send Gabriel if she finds incriminating evidence. ('I've just had the worst day at my mother's. I'd love to see you.') But it doesn't matter anyway – there's Archan's favourite mug on the second shelf. Blue, with a stencil of Misa from *Death Note*.

'I'll come back when the boys are here,' says Kolia, and she leaves.

5.

Almost as soon as she's home, Kolia has to get ready to go out again. It's only noon but it feels like she's lived ten days since breakfast, so she shakes a Vyvanse out of its brown bottle without thinking too hard about it.

She showers quickly and scarfs some leftover takeaway from two days ago. There's a single pomegranate in the fruit bowl. She'd bought it on a whim earlier that week, surprised at how cheap it was. With one eye on the clock, Kolia sets about halving it. She doesn't want to think about the two options, that her brothers were lying or her brothers were scared; she doesn't want to think about much. She deserves the same superfood that Enzo spends all day getting spoon-fed.

When the pomegranate falls apart, Kolia feels like laughing. It's all pith and membrane, a few paltry clusters of seed clinging to the mesocarp like her dad's eyebrows. She goes at it with a teaspoon and the seeds come out almost one at a time, either unpleasantly smashed by the spoon or with clumps of the bitter, woody white still attached. She eats each one as soon as it's loose and is serially underwhelmed.

What a joke. On the train to work, she looks up how M&S shell their pomegranate seeds. Google shows her a deseeding machine, blue and fast: a spiky, slatted, wire-mother looking contraption. Poor Devna. The pomegranate as a symbol needs to move away from all that Twitter-poetry, life-and-death, Hades-and-Persephone shit, Kolia thinks; it should just symbol-ise work. Next time she wants to do something nice for herself, she'll pick something less labour intensive.

She can tell when the Vyvanse kicks in because her chewing gum has suddenly disintegrated and her teeth are sore. She doesn't make a habit of taking it but she's familiar with the trajectory: a glittering surge of energy for a few hours and then a dullness. It helps when the prospect of dealing with Enzo becomes overpowering. Kolia had been an unhinged kid once too but differently unhinged. She remembers as the train pulls into her station: mad little Kolia, setting discreet fires and cutting herself and having an imaginary friend into late teen-hood. (Oh, she doesn't want to ever talk to her mother again.)

Enzo's waiting at the table in the yellow kitchen when she arrives. He smiles angelically, mouth full of red like he's been chewing small animals. Francesca's not there, thank god. Kolia sits down beside him, full of chemical pep.

'Hi Enzo! How was your weekend?! We're going to do a full test paper today, okay, exam-style. You can still ask me questions but we're going to try and do it timed. Does that sound okay?'

Enzo nods. 'Can you ask Devna to make me a golden milk?'

'Of course I can.' Kolia ruffles his hair. 'You get started.'

While Enzo tries to figure out how many ducks are on a pond if there are two ducks in front of a duck, two ducks behind a duck and a duck in the middle, Kolia approaches the kitchen island.

'Hi Devna. Um, could you tell me what's in a golden milk and I'll make him one?'

'It's just cashew milk with turmeric, cinnamon, honey. I'll make it.'

'You don't have to do that,' says Kolia brightly. 'Let me.' Really, most people who deal with kids should be allowed amphetamines.

Devna looks at her almost approvingly; certainly with the most warmth Kolia's ever seen. 'I'll make it. Do you want one?'

'Thank you, that's so kind.' Beaming, she returns to Enzo, who's pushing his lip out with concentration. Care is work, she thinks, and work should be compensated. She turns the page for him. Sixty pounds an hour. 'You're doing really well, Enzo. Keep it up!'

It's going smoothly until the golden milk arrives, at which point he becomes absorbed in attempting to drink from the wrong side of the cup. Kolia tries not to let this annoy her but her heightened alertness makes every slurp piercing. He refuses gleefully when she asks him to stop.

'Okay,' she says eventually. 'If you don't get back to work, I'm going to take the milk away.'

'No!' screams Enzo, and he tips the cup over and barrels out of the room.

Kolia nods to herself. Her hands are icy in the warm afternoon, which must be something to do with the Vyvanse, and also she's filled with rage. She controls it: she doesn't run until she's out of the kitchen.

She chases Enzo into his bedroom. He giggles, pants happily, bounces on the balls of his tiny feet on the other side of the bed, waiting for her to pounce. It takes a second for Kolia to register that she hasn't been in this room before, only in his brother's. Actually, she'd read his brother bedtime stories. Enzo's room is huge and adorable, with foam cut-outs shaped like different dinosaurs on the walls. There are wall-to-wall shelves filled with children's books, board games, models, markers; he has an alarm clock shaped like a ladybird on his bedside table, and a display box full of quartz and amethyst and tiger's eye. Kolia feels suddenly heavy, like the come-down dullness has descended early. Enzo's still giggling maniacally across the room. She thinks of the Baby and his geezerish ways, Archan and his unbroken cup. *My brothers would eat you up, white boy*, she thinks. It's not a phrase that comes naturally.

Kolia lunges across the bed and grabs him by the shoulders. He doesn't struggle, just looks up at her with a silly smile. She's still wired but now she's heavy too, with everything from this morning that she can't think about. Her mother's guileless smile. Her mother saying, 'Kids lie.' Saying, 'I thought he might hit me'. Before she knows what she's doing, Kolia's taken the scissors out of Enzo's boutique desk organiser, yellow and green for left-handed. She holds him firm with the other hand and then she's cutting madly, hacking away at his perfect ringlets.

He doesn't shout or resist; he's still grinning like he wants to get the joke. There are curls all over the carpet.

Devna gasps when they get downstairs. Enzo had been a cherub five minutes ago, tipping over his golden milk: almost twenty per cent ringlets. Now his hair's in ugly hanks, with a patch at the side that's almost bald.

'Look what Kolia did to my hair,' he says roguishly.

Kolia's jaw drops. 'Enzo, that's a horrible thing to say.' She turns to Devna, concern in her eyes. 'I found him cutting his hair upstairs. I tried to stop it but I was worried about grabbing the scissors away.'

'That's not true!' shrieks Enzo, scrambling up on the counter. He's still shedding whole locks of hair that had been cut but not fallen. More than ever, he resembles a child that might join forces with the Babadook.

Devna shakes her head. 'Oh Enzo,' she says, but she's looking at Kolia. 'Your mother's going to be very unhappy.'

6.

Kolia's too shaken by the guerilla haircut incident to work on a proper snare for Gabriel. She walks around her flat in circles, thinking of her grip on the little boy's shoulder, of how suddenly she'd snapped. How Lalita-like, and worse, how satisfying – the flash and saw of silver scissors . . .

She doesn't have the time to deploy coy and veiled hints at home trouble. She gets his attention the old-fashioned way: abrupt shift in tone, slower responses, emoji embargo. Two days later, he's 'thinking of her'; the next evening, he's slipping his hand into her jeans in front of *The Sopranos*.

Kolia pulls away, aware she hasn't washed the day off yet. Gabriel smiles at her. She wishes they could touch in more and littler ways, sexless ways. A white woman in the queue for the post office screamed at her that morning. She wants to know that if she tells him about it, he'll pull her into his arms.

'I've been thinking about your milk kink,' she says instead.

'I wouldn't think too hard about it.'

'You don't want me meditating on its origins?'

She looks up at the wall behind the sofa they've been sitting on. The well-known ceramicist has furnished her son with another piece: an empty frame swarming with disorderly calves and thighs, the frame-corner itself melting into an uncanny ankle bone.

'It exists in a void, I'm pretty sure.'

Kolia's not even sure how she would facilitate the fantasy, short of actual sexually induced lactation (one of the mysteries she encountered during her research, after which she'd felt a psychosomatic prickling from inside her bra for hours). Gabriel tells her that it's not about nursing. He wants to drink it, he wants it on his lip, he wants it in his face. They discuss the possibility that it's a gender-flipped cum fantasy, and then they stop talking about it.

When they have sex, Kolia asks him to hold her tighter. She'd frozen up when the woman at the post office had shouted at her. She'd felt very young. Gabriel's hand is on the cushion next to her face. A few strands of her hair are caught in his fingers. It hurts a tiny bit, until it doesn't. Kolia's thoughts become smaller and smaller until they're suddenly undefined and transportive. She's losing herself again to the walls, the cistern, the damp fridge, until she can see the bare dining table. All the chairs are occupied now.

Kolia's hands are at the head of the table. They cross over each other like legs and share a single seat. Her neck is at the other end of the table. It's easier to recognise as her own than her hands are, actually. Her breasts sit opposite each other.

Something about the configuration – four seats at a square table facing each other like card players – reminds Kolia of a stage setting. Carver by Birdman. She feels like the body parts could break into an am-dram version of *Who's Afraid of Virginia Woolf?* at any minute. They speak in pieces, throw little lies out. Neck thinks that the water in this apartment tastes old, tastes like bathroom water even when it comes out of the kitchen sink. Right Hand says that she wishes Eyes could have made it to the dinner. Left Hand tells the breasts sitting either side of her that she was reading about a new magazine committed entirely to nipple beauty and sponsored by The Body Shop. The girls are talking to each other only. They mutter about alcoholic prosthetists and bellfounders and Ludmila Ulitskaya burying her own mastectomised breast in a burial ground consecrated for amputated appendages: 'Perhaps only a first instalment!'

It's not unusual for Kolia to be distracted by visions during sex. Intrusive images of sword swallowers, people in the corner of the room, a head laid flat out on an ice rink about to be dissected by someone going too fast. It's always the closeness she finds gratifying rather than the physical touch. Words of affirmation get her going. At her worst, Kolia feels completely detached from sex. She wants only – love. Why does she have to keep this a secret when he can look her in the eye and happily tell her every specific, lipidic detail of what he'd like? Kolia was impressed and surprised when Gabriel first told her that he also suffered from intrusive thoughts, but it turned out he meant more like wanting to push toddlers over when they were in front of him walking too slowly. But she's never had a disloca-tion as clear as this . . . She kisses Gabriel back when he asks her to and the appendages are still in front of her, sat at the table. She's disembodied and embodied five times over.

'You just don't seem like you're into it,' Gabriel's saying. 'You're shaking.'

He's right; she's very slightly trembling. 'I'm into it,' she re-assures him. She goes too far; she promises him that she's enjoy-ing herself so fervently that he becomes even more disconcerted (though he pushes manfully on).

Afterwards, he hands her a towel and she can feel that some-thing's gone wrong. She waits to be told whether she can stay the night; she has to stop herself from following him into the bathroom. Instead, she circles his apartment, listening to him piss, picking things up off the shelves because her hands seem very empty. This is exactly how her youngest brother acts when their mother takes a call. Lalita breastfed him for three times as long as the others and it shows. He was sleeping in her bed most nights until he was eight. He's only recently stopped using a two-pound coin to open the toilet door from the outside so that she can't keep them apart. He's also, bizarrely, better adjusted than either Kolia or Archan were at his age: happy, popular, hard-working.

This thought – the Baby, small and milk-fed – and the recent sex combine oddly for Kolia. She notices that she's still shaking, a twitch where Gabriel had skimmed her hips with his. She thinks of her brother telling fibs about his broken mug; she thinks of Sicily, ten years ago.

Gabriel comes out of the bathroom and goes straight to her. He hasn't cleaned the soap suds off himself properly; she can smell tea-tree when he puts his arms around her.

'You shower, I'll cook?'

'I'm staying over?'

'Obviously.' He connects to the speaker, music for cooking, Louis Armstrong.

Kolia's so touched by the 'obviously' that she doesn't mention Sicily – even when Gabriel tells poignant, funny stories about his parents' divorce over wine at dinner; even when there's a gap in their conversation perfect for her Italian tragicomedy. But she thinks about it later, under the duvet. The skin at her hip stuttering.

And the songs that Gabriel had played, Louis Armstrong, 'A Foggy Day', catching in her head, reeling ten years ago closer.

The song, the skin at her hip, stuttering like film stuck in a projector.

7.

Sicily

Lalita had been a jazz singer once.

It was one of a rotation of facts that Kolia had fixed on, back when she was still delighted by her mother's unfiltered sharing. She'd been a jazz singer, she'd been a classical dancer, she'd been proposed to by a man with a ring where the ruby was shaped like a heart. She'd kept company with anarchists and she'd got naked on a horse called Physical Energy in Hyde Park. There's an undeniable glamour to Lalita's early years. Perhaps the glamour's just a natural result of narrator bias, but Kolia considers it more likely that the things that make Lalita unbearable now (total self-belief, total lack of self-awareness or self-consciousness) simply suited her better when she was young. That's a bad thing to think, Kolia knows. It's that same old foible, a feeling like misogyny which sometimes overtakes her when she looks at her mother.

(But bohemianism does age badly, everyone knows that. A while after Lalita separated from the boys' father, she took up with a man that reminded her of the free-love London garrets she'd associated with at university. He didn't look like an anarchist to Kolia. He was pale, plump, in his forties with receding hair and weak, watery eyes. He was in the habit of walking around the house with no clothes on. When Kolia objected he scolded her for having such a Victorian attitude towards nudity.

'He's a free soul, like me,' Lalita told her.

She demonstrated her free and unboundaried ways by involving him immediately and totally in Kolia's life. When Kolia was caught watching pornography, they lectured her as a couple. When she felt little nodules coming through behind her nipples and thought she had cancer, Lalita had her undress in the front room and asked the new boyfriend for his opinion. 'Probably a cyst,' he opined, scholarly.

'Do you love him more than me, Mum?' Kolia had asked one day. She only asked because she knew there was only one answer; she knew her mother would have to say, no, of course not, I could never love anything as much as I love you.

'You can't control who you love, darling,' Lalita had said.)

These days there's dry skin all round Lalita's bohemian face and when she scratches it, it rasps. It would be horrible now, for her to get naked on a horse.

It was ten years ago that Kolia last saw her mother's jazz singer. Lalita went to Sicily shortly after her father's funeral, for another visit to the Palermo state archives. She'd installed herself at a hotel in Cefalù for the week, with four-year-old Archan and an awestruck pupil barrister. Then, unlimited in her bounty, she'd surprised Kolia with tickets to join them for the weekend.

It was early summer. School had basically ground to a halt and Kolia was fifteen. Carefully, alone, she made it through Heathrow and then held her breath the whole way to Cefalù, where she was met by the beaming intern. They sunbathed on warm, dry stones on an empty beach, and Lalita dared Kolia to swim.

'I don't have a swimsuit.'

'Go naked, no one's here,' said Lalita. 'You're only young once, you know. If I had your body, I'd never put clothes on.'

The intern stared, wide-eyed, like she couldn't believe how cool a mother of three could be.

She was odd, the intern, almost dopey. Kolia could tell she thought she'd lucked out, between the free flights and the hotel and the awe she showed Lalita – apparently without noticing that she'd been stuck with all the admin and most of the child-care. In this way, she was like most of Lalita's waifs, adopted under the guise of care, seamlessly manipulated into free labour.

(Even by fifteen Kolia had noticed the pattern. Helping people was Lalita's life duty: she couldn't stop herself, and usually it went one of two ways. In some cases, she'd help them at the cost of others or to the point of no return. The MSF volunteer she'd met on Tinder, for example, who was so trau-matised from volunteering in Palestine that he couldn't work. She gave him all of Kolia's savings; he disappeared with the television. Later, of course, it came out that he'd never been on the MSF books. In other cases, she'd help them, and they'd pay her back. The Nadars had been sleeping on an airport floor when Lalita invited them to live with her; they ran odd jobs in return, grocery runs and deliveries. She hadn't been able to kick them out in the end and was always finding the grandpa in her room in the middle of the night.)

The intern was in her early twenties. She was Kurdish, want-ing to specialise in Kurdish human rights, and a passionate cosplayer, even bringing her outfit to Sicily – some latex-and-tulle bit of elfish garb that Kolia spotted at the back of her suit-case. Both Kurdishness and cosplay made sense: anything that could tip her into identifying as an outsider played directly into Lalita's hands, and so there she was, gulping up the hype, buried in admin and childcare, like the Nadars had been, like Kolia sometimes was. Admin and childcare: Lalita's two pet hates.

The day they visited the archives, the intern was left behind in Cefalù, billing old cases. She didn't express disappointment. It was an hour's train to Palermo anyway.

Lalita had looked perfect, walking through the Sicilian heat. Like a powerful European matriarch on an HBO show. Dark hair packed up in a black open turban, loose cream wrap dress. She'd moved with authority, impervious to the heat, noise, strangeness. At her side, Archan's anxiety was through the roof. Even at four, he was nervous, shy. Kolia saw that it was getting under his skin that they were walking three abreast down the narrow romance streets. He dropped awkwardly down to walk in the gutter every time an Italian even looked at him. Kolia caught him by the hand and dragged him back a couple of paces, and they walked like that together until they reached the archives. Outside the building, which looked like a rundown hotel, Lalita turned to assess her children. 'Soprintendenza Archivistica della Sicilia,' she intoned, arms outspread, rolling the Rs and trilling the Ls. Kolia rolled her eyes and Archan rolled his too.

The state archives of Palermo had been built to house historical records of souls and goods. 'And to this day, it's updated with the registries of souls,' Lalita whispered as they passed through. The building was prettier on the inside, built around a central courtyard with a fountain. Orange fish swam in olive-green water. The entrance hall was covered with ornate, unpainted plasterwork: expressionless babies and naked youths. The souls, Kolia supposed.

At the entrance to records room, they were met by an Italian man, who had them sign in.

'You need help?' he asked them.

'No, thank you so much.'

'You don't speak Italian,' Kolia reminded her mother.

'You can't underestimate boots on the ground, darling. Anyway, there's no reading Italian – it's all numbers. I'm just looking for the right year. I find the years, I find the dates, I find the months.'

The records room wasn't grand. It was empty and musky, shaped like a barn. The windows were fitted with jadeite panels to keep the sunlight out; there was something plasticky about them, a trace of eighties office catalogue. Lalita marched along the shelves, occasionally taking a couple of steps up a ladder. The heavy, warm silence was broken by her translation app, which sounded every few minutes.

After half an hour, Lalita had found the census she needed. She headed towards the adjoining room, which was filled with scholars making their way through impossibly valuable books. 'Excuse me,' called the man who'd signed them in. 'You need to register which book you take to the reading room.'

'I know,' Lalita said, changing direction. 'I've been here before.'

Kolia hadn't forgotten the last time Lalita had gone to Palermo. She hadn't forgotten Nino, even if she hadn't thought about him in a while. She did a dozen slow rounds of the shelves while her mother read, careful on each step to avoid her sandal-backs making a sound on the marble. Warm, dim, historic. It ought to be the perfect place to think of Nino, really put in the hours, concentrate on him the way she hadn't for years. And all the material of Sicily so far – statues, temples, myths of love and violence on every surface (in the middle of fountains and on the ceilings of restaurants) – had sharpened her sense for fantasy, so that she was ready to summon up Nino and project him immediately into an imagined framework of sex and loss and blood. But Kolia wasn't as good at losing herself as she'd been when she was younger, and every time she finished a lap of the bookshelves the man who'd signed them in was there, smiling at her.

Back outside the archives, the sun was beating down. Archan was dragging his feet, ready to go home. Sicily so far had been beautiful but taxing. Lalita had been holding forth all holiday about how this was the island where Persephone had lived with

Demeter before Hades snatched her away and where she returned every spring and summer. This is where Persephone removed her belt of flowers; this is where she floated them downriver, as a message for her mother to get help. Lalita talks at Kolia adoringly all the way through the Valley of Temples: 'It's a story about how missing your daughter can turn the world into winter.' Kolia had imagined Persephone being psyched to get to Hades, the way that she'd once longed to go to boarding school.

Even after the long morning at the archives, Lalita was so amped up on the beauty of everything that they missed the train to their hotel. She wandered into a dozen shops and considered the aubergines in the vegetable stalls and translated posters for long-gone music festivals on her phone. They walked around waiting for the next train, which was in an hour; except Lalita had misremembered the schedule time and they showed up for that one five minutes too late. Kolia suggested they wait at the station café so that there would be no chance of missing the next one, but that was wasting the day, and this gave them the perfect chance to check out an atelier Lalita's client had recommended! They got lost on the way back from the bakery and missed the third train.

It was 2 p.m. at that point and still midday bright, and they had been walking for two hours. Archan was getting visibly frustrated. Heat always made him anxious. He looked at the ground, ignoring all of Lalita's conversation-starters and her comments about Palermo, until suddenly, she snapped.

'I'm sorry,' she said, not sounding it, in a kind of hissing roar that made them jump. They were in the middle of the street. Archan tried to move into the shadows, out of the way, out of sight, but there were no shadows to be found. 'I'm sorry,' she said again. 'I'm sorry that I've brought you on this beautiful holiday. I'm sorry that I have to be saving lives. Shall I pull a train for you out of my arsehole?' (A passer-by said something Italian in response to this and Archan looked like he wanted to die.) 'You have no idea how lucky you are to be here. Do you know what happened to the man whose records we found today? Did you see my papers? He was raped with a soda bottle. It exploded inside him. It ruptured his organs.' Archan was crying now. He'd fallen down against the hot wall, just under a peeling poster about saints and orchestras.

They had nearly two hours now before the next train pulled into Palermo Centrale. They ducked into a doorway advertising cold drinks. The indoor seating was being refurbished, explained a beautiful woman, and she led them into a courtyard. The whitewashed stone and a couple of tall plants provided some shade but the bench on which Kolia and Archan sat was in direct blazing sun. They ordered juices; the beautiful woman brought over a snack because they looked so tired. Archan had retreated into himself now, wasn't saying a word. Kolia wondered if he knew what raped meant. After a short silence, the sound of an outdoor speaker starting up. She hadn't noticed it standing in the corner of the courtyard. She imagined the beautiful woman watching them from somewhere inside the restaurant and deciding that what the miserable family in the courtyard needed was some music.

The song that played was jazz. 'So In Love', Kolia recognized after a while; it was a song her mother used to sing. The singer was singing in English, and the speaker seemed to be playing impossibly loudly.

'Cole Porter,' said Lalita loudly over the music. 'This version is Ella Fitzgerald's, but it's Cole Porter's song.'

She started singing.

When Lalita had sung this to Kolia when she was little, she'd thought the lyrics were about strange deer, true deer. She'd fall asleep in a jazz lullaby dreamland: birds singing in the sycamore tree and sycamore-tree forests full of three-eyed stags. Pennies from heaven, upturned umbrellas. Fish jumping up to catch high curtains in their mouths. But this was loud.

Archan had his hands over his head, shaking. Kolia tried to appear fully absorbed in her complimentary biscotti, smiling in weak approval when her mother turned to her. Lalita was singing directly to Kolia now, serenading her. Deafening noise, boiling heat . . . Lalita in her turban from the twenties, swaying side to side. Existing in this picture of herself – Palermo: Episode 2.

Archan had become non-verbal. Kolia put a hand on his back but he didn't seem to like it; he was making noises, rocking. Lalita kept singing. Like she couldn't even see him.

They took a taxi back to the hotel in the end.

Under the duvet, Gabriel presses his foot back, tucks it between her calves. The sex had reminded her of Sicily, the disembodiment; but it isn't the beach or the archives that it's bringing to mind. There's something else – there had been something else.

On their last night in Sicily, Lalita wanted to go out.

'Carousing,' she called it. 'Look at us, three beautiful women. Why aren't we carousing?'

Because she wanted the intern by her side, she dialled up the taxi driver who'd driven them back from Palermo. He was in his fifties and didn't speak much English, but did agree to watch Archan while his mother caroused.

'I'll give you a big tip,' Lalita said, making the sign, fingers rubbing together. The gesture made Kolia cringe, but she hadn't thought twice back then about leaving the four-year-old with a stranger. The intern had promised to do Kolia's eyeliner for her and she was wearing one of her mother's dresses.

They started in a bar with a huge wall mirror. Lalita let Kolia have a glass of champagne and she watched their three reflections. The intern was slightly offbeat, with her fuchsia cardigan and the cartoon-character tattoo peeking out at the sleeve, but there they were: three beautiful women. Later they went to a dark blue room with a dancefloor, which Lalita kept calling a discotheque. 'Dance, come on,' she called out to Kolia. 'You're so beautiful! Dance!'

It was the third club they'd tried because the first two had asked for ID. Lalita said it didn't matter but Kolia felt even younger than fifteen in the blue room. Especially when people looked at her, especially when men looked at her, especially when men danced with her, especially when they held her by the hips and wouldn't let her spin away. She looked around for help but her mum was nodding encouragingly at her. She opened her eyes wide to say help and her mum raised her eyebrows back, gave her a thumbs up. Now his hand was further down. Now – in a flash of fuchsia, the intern took her by the hand.

'Do you want some water?' she asked.

They went over to the bar where Lalita was sipping a Schweppes.

'Did you see that?' Kolia asked her mother.

She nodded. 'He's very handsome, isn't he? No less than you deserve, darling.'

Later, Lalita told her that the thing with virginity was just to get rid of it as soon as possible. Kolia knew about her mother and the horse called Physical Energy and was beginning to understand what bohemianism was. That was what had just happened to her, in the blue room in the shadow of the mountain: bohemianism.

8.

Kolia pushes her face into Gabriel's back. She hasn't thought about Sicily in years. She remembers how it felt to get back to the hotel room and see her brother safely asleep and the taxi driver watching *The Simpsons*, volume down, subtitles on.

'What are you thinking about?' says Gabriel.

'I thought you were asleep.'

'I was. You keep shaking your leg.'

'Oh. Sorry.'

He turns around to face her. He's beautiful like this, sleep still on him, a crease on his cheek from the pillow. When he says he can feel her worrying, warmth envelops her: the feeling of being known and cared for. He asks again what she's thinking about.

'Just. What I'm going to do now, I guess. I don't think I'm going to be asked back to teach Enzo.'

As soon as she says it, it all comes back, the anger, the fallen hanks of hair. She can't ever return, she realises, even if Devna's strangely on side. Her safe, dull job is scorched earth.

Gabriel laughs without opening his eyes. 'Plenty of seven-year-olds in the sea.'

'Yeah, I guess.' Ahead of her, spreading empty days with no money. 'I always thought it would be more of a stopgap job anyway. It's not exactly fulfilling.'

'Work rarely is. Something to do with late capitalism.'

'I want to do something. Obviously. But something good.'

Gabriel hums his agreement.

'Like my mum is a terrible, terrible role model, of course.' Kolia pauses. 'But she has a purpose. And passion.'

'Like of the Christ,' says Gabriel. Kolia huffs and turns on her side, but he rolls her back over to face him. His eyes are open now, sincere and enthusiastic. 'Why don't you work at your grandma's school? Seriously. Quit your job, move over there for a year, see how you like it. It's like a ready-made mission.'

The warmth dissolves. Kolia works to hide her unhappiness. Gabriel doesn't care whether she's in the country or not; Gabriel doesn't want to be with her; Gabriel would be happy for her to disappear for a year. It's Kolia's fault for talking about the school over dinner. Really she'd been showing off, the same way she sometimes shows off about her mother's job to people who don't know Lalita well (my family are agents of change; I've been raised with a cause) and she likes to mention that her grandmother has a school over there because it strengthens her connection with a country that she otherwise knows little about. It's a habit to which she's especially susceptible when talking to white people, particularly if they're attractive: some convoluted flex that compels Kolia to assert the superiority of her intricate and storied background in comparison to their staid ancestries. Rather than being speechless with interest, Gabriel had nodded like it made a lot of sense for Kolia's grandmother to have started a school in her home village. Now he's drifting back off, happy with his sensible suggestion that Kolia teach there. Kolia exhales, tries to commit to sleep. Slowly, her discontent bleeds away. The gnawing necessity of avoiding Francesca remains. And on Gabriel's grey, pilly sheets, the idea grows on her until it develops into a kind of epiphany.

*

She's only heard awful things about the country's recent history but the school looks quite lovely. It's tucked into the outskirts of a town in the north and built around a deep, manmade fishing lake. There are red macaws, a little tugboat. Kids running around, looking more like her brothers than like Enzo. A million gods, gold, fruit and flowers and washing with milk; an ineffable sense of purpose. Kolia wouldn't need to speak the language, her grandmother says; their volunteer teachers come from all over. But maybe she could learn it. Inevitably she would learn about her inheritance, historical, genetic. It would be nice not to be the 'whitest brown person' that some blonde bitch at a party knows, and nice to know more about her own gods than which one to pray to when you lose something, which ones for good grades.

She's ready for reality, for specific understanding rather than this patchwork of suggestion and trope. Nino had been one of her strongest links to her mother's country, and he was imaginary. When she'd pictured herself there, she pictured him too: the two of them recuperating from their respective traumas, his wounds fading by the sea. She has a vision of him now, laughing, opening his shirt so that she can see his burns. They're raw, like his mother made them yesterday and not when he was seven. He's laughing at her. What's your trauma to mine? What are you doing about it? (She'd burned herself with a cigarette once, on purpose, when she was fifteen. She hadn't been thinking of Nino at the time but she did afterwards, when it bubbled and swelled, and even now sometimes she thinks of him when she sees it, a little half-moon scar.) He's laughing at her, at all the secrets she's told him. 'It's so hard being the daughter of a lawyer,' he mocks, drawing out the 'so'. He's handsome when he laughs. The burn marks are seething under his skin. 'Poor baby. Do you need to go cry about the black-and-white backs of photocopier paper? That's my black-and-white back. Your mother works every day to save me. What do you do? What have you ever done, except for sit here and imagine me holding your hand? Do something, you fucker.' *Yes*, Kolia thinks. She wants to do something, finally, the way her mother does; the way her mother always has.

In the morning Kolia asks Gabriel if he knows that he smiles during sex. She's never met anyone who does that before. He tells her that he smiles whenever he's happy. It blows Kolia's mind. There's literally nothing more complex than that going on, no necessary diffusion of one emotion into ten more nuanced emotions and thirty different reactions. He sees, he smiles; what a prince. She briefly imagines sitting at dinner with his mother, who always keeps the fridge well-stocked. She wonders if he lied about not having finished *The Grapes of Wrath*.

Kolia tells him he can suck on her tit. She combs her hands through his hair. He says intimate, embarrassing things. Kolia doesn't float away. All twenty-one grams of the soul stay bodied. She's tethered, momentarily, by an imaginary current running from her body to his.

PART 4: A SIGN FROM GOD

1.

In a dark blue hour when the air is still cool, after the blackbirds have started singing but before the sun is up, Sheba noses at the back door. It's been left slightly ajar; it opens easily when she pushes her head into it. The dog ignores the patchy lawn and wanders round the side of the house to the front yard, following the damp undergrowth smell of the hedge, whining quietly at the iron gate. She can smell foxes.

Upstairs, Lalita wakes up with a sense of clean, gentle energy, expanding in her chest like a bubble. She stretches deeply, raising her arms to the ceiling and then circling them down. Her fingertips reach higher and wider than they usually do. She continues, pushing her chest forward, her shoulder blades together, making space for the energy, letting it announce its direction.

Kolia had been by three days earlier to check in. The boys must have complained after an argument about the console. Lalita didn't mind. It was good for Kolia to see how well she was doing, to see that she had nothing to hide. The thought excites the bubble in her chest. She wants to spread it through the whole house, that feeling of nothing to hide. A fresh start; Kolia, back at last – a hundred plans suggest themselves. The master bedroom's the place to start, of course. It makes no sense to keep it locked up, and there's always been something horrible about that dead space at the end of the corridor, something unhealthy. It's a feng shui nightmare: a circulatory issue, like one shut-off artery or frostbitten finger. The whole soul of the house will be improved; Kolia can have her own room.

It takes longer than expected to break the door down. Lalita had thought she'd use a hammer but the toolbox is rusted shut, so she uses the toolbox itself instead, swinging it into the panel above the doorknob. She feels productive, feels powerful. She's Mrs Dalloway, taking the doors off their hinges! Both panels have been reduced to splinters when she realises the boys are watching from the other end of the hall. They're confused, still half asleep; it's early even for a school day. But it's good for them to be awake, up with the sun, which is right now washing the garden in pale gold.

The look on Archan's face bothers her. She's seen this particular expression a few times since the argument about their console: concern, wary fear. For him to look at Lalita like he's scared of her confirms how sheltered he's been. She'd only ever have made that face at her father if he'd been about to hit her. Still, the bubble of energy is silvery and gracious; she improvises a solution without effort.

'I'm working on a big project. Can you stay home and help me, Archan?'

His face changes immediately. 'I don't have to go to school?'

'No, not today.' He hates going to school, she knows. It's his anxiety. Sometimes his stomach gets so bad from it that he has to stay home anyway. 'I have something more enriching for you. Something for your artistic sensibilities.'

Archan fetches the oven glove so she can break off the bigger splinters. The Baby rubs his eyes and goes back to bed.

Once she's made enough of a hole to put her arm through, Lalita opens the door from the other side. She takes in the room for a second. A pair of forgotten headphones is the only indication of Kolia's recent stay; otherwise it looks the same as it has for fifteen years. She signals to Archan, who lays down a supermarket bag in which he's been collecting the pieces of broken door and follows her to a huge, low butler's desk made of dark wood.

'This bureau. Can you help me move it down the hall?'

While he drags it across the carpet, she marches ahead, pulls the duvet off the Baby.

'We're going to do a project in your room, okay? Can you put newspaper down?'

'We don't have any newspaper,' he points out.

Lalita rushes back, out of breath, pulls the drawers out of the desk. She empties them across the floor of the dichondra room, the long space between the boys' two beds. Their contents thump and feather out. The Baby lifts out the heavier things, photo albums, matchboxes, and puts them neatly on the console table. Then he spreads the documents from inside the folders evenly over the floor. The paper rucks and tears as Archan tries to set the desk down.

'We're going to do a tabletop mural. You're going to paint it, Archan.'

He nods seriously.

'Anything you want.'

Lalita takes the stairs as fast as she can, gathers up supplies from when she'd planned to do the garden shed: sandpaper, paint tins. Her breathing's laboured but she's buoyed up by the greatness of her idea. Archan's studying the desk, which is low and pretty. Dark wood, thin layer of dust. Art's very good for anxiety, she's read.

*

The morning passes quickly. The Baby puts out food for Sheba but doesn't have time to find her for a cuddle before he has to leave for school. Lalita darts around the master bedroom, working out which other pieces of furniture she wants to rehabilitate. Archan sands down the table.

He goes to get Lalita when he's finished, stands outside the room. A stale, brown smell escapes into the hallway; the smell of old air meeting new air. There's that caution in his eyes again.

'You should open the windows, Mum. You're raising all the dust.'

She is. It's not clear how, with her spindly arms and slow heaviness, but she's been tossing around the furniture in here like a strongman. The wardrobe's on its side; a shelving unit's fallen over, scattering letters, books, more photo albums. There's dark-wood wreckage everywhere and overspill in the hallway, loose drawers at Archan's feet.

'It's all dust,' says Lalita. 'Which is skin, did you know? I've been meaning to do one of those allergen tests for my scratching and I already know it would tell me I'm allergic to dust. And pollen, and horses, maybe even Sheba, but especially dust. Which is everywhere. And which means I'm allergic to skin. Which explains a lot.' On every 'which' she disorders the room a step further – pulls clothes off their hangers, sweeps clear a side-table, throws back the dusty duvet. The movements seem almost inhuman. There's something uncanny and automatic about the way she's talking, too. Archan's frightened, though it's not unusual for Lalita to be impassioned like this: the fire, cackle, darting. Long, noisy scratches down the side of her arms.

'I'm going to start painting, okay?'

'Okay,' she says.

'Anything I want?'

She stops to face him, wobbling on her feet a little, like she's just come off a ride. 'Actually, I have a starting vision for you to work around.' He knows how important her space is, she says. And how nice it is not having any men in the house, how it means everything can be as pretty as she wants it. 'No men except for you, of course. My sweetest man.'

Lalita's starting vision is a Japanese theme, 'orchids, some birds, some cherry blossom'. She does more research while her coffee brews and, once Archan has put down the base layer and made some sketches, she jumps in again.

'Could you design something around "vulning"? It's a heraldic symbol. Like on a family crest, you know, or a coat of arms. I think it would be so clever if you could.' She's liked the idea since a medieval history module at university, she explains. In the Middle Ages, it was thought that pelicans fed their young with their own blood and 'vulning' was the name for when they wounded themselves. 'Pecking at their own breast until they were hurt enough to feed. So in iconography, it can represent family or it can be the sacrifice of Christ. Wouldn't it be cool if we had a family crest?'

Archan nods. She knew he'd love it. All her children tend towards high concept. Already he's sketching, reworking the idea to fit with the Japanese theme so that rather than a pelican it's a crane, twining down its long, calligraphic neck to self-mutilate.

2.

The Baby gets in from school and bolts up the stairs to see what progress has been made. The room stinks of Dulux but he stays to keep the artist company; he sits at the computer and makes his Wood Elf run in circles. Archan can't hide how pleased he is when they call Lalita in to see the finished product.

'It's good . . .' She examines it intently. 'You can really tell that you watch a lot of anime. It needs some changes though.'

He wants to strop at this, she can tell, but he makes the corrections with a delicate hand. Brighter blossom, darker stamens, another bud where Lalita thought the orchids looked lopsided. She gives it another look, sucking on the cotton candy vape.

'I don't think it makes sense for there to be floating blossoms *above* the tree. They'd float down, wouldn't they? Because of gravity.'

'Mum, you're so annoying.' Archan's getting himself worked up now. 'I've painted a breeze.'

'Don't speak to me like that. If you're going to do something, do it well. Stop leaning into your laziness.'

'I don't want to do this any more.'

Lalita can hear in his voice that he's close to tears. She can't stand crying over nothing. She heads downstairs where her iPad's chiming, sits down to unlock it. The Baby stays at the gaming table, pinching the ends of his fingers, but Archan follows her.

'I want to go to Dad's house,' he says. The usual recourse. When she doesn't respond, he presses his hand through the struts at the side of the nursing chair to poke at her leg. Lalita bats him away. She's scrolling through reams of dense text with narrowed, focused eyes.

'Can I text Dad?'

'Something's not right,' says Lalita. She pulls again on her vape, swipes to another tab. 'The Bar Standards Board moved my hearing up. They never do that. I have cases in motion that they said would not be affected.'

'Oh,' says Archan. 'I'm sorry.' The look in his eyes again, like he's scared of her. Why does everyone act like she's something to be scared of?

'It's such a one-off thing,' she says, her hand sharp and furious on the trackpad. 'One journalist, one supposed violation. It's not like I'm unfit to practise. It's not like I'm going to court fucked. It's not like I'm losing cases, even.'

'Do you think someone's said something to get it moved up? The guy at your work that you don't like any more—'

'It wouldn't be someone from chambers. We're close. We fight, but it's like a family fighting. And anyway, I bring all the money in.'

'What's his name though, Mum, the man you don't like? He could be their inside guy.'

Lalita looks up, finally. 'Yash's family is from my mother's village. Our fathers were batchmates. It doesn't matter if he likes me. We just finished a case together, the kid of a woman from the same village. We literally stopped them as they were putting this boy on the plane.'

'Yeah, you believe in stuff like that – blood-ties stuff, and bonding by fire – but not everyone else does.'

Lalita's eyes are firmly back on the screen. She's not listening any more; she plugs at her vape. 'You don't know what you're talking about, so don't pretend. Chambers is behind me. I'm in the Legal 500. They should be scared of me, the fuckers.'

Archan's stung. 'I'm sure they are scared of you,' he says, as cruel as he can manage.

She can feel the voice starting in her teeth before it comes out of her. Mean and thin and sharp. 'Get out. Right now. I've had all I can take of you today. This isn't just about my life, you know, or even your life, or the money that puts food in your ungrateful mouth. It's other people, life and death. Go on, fuck off.'

Archan runs out. He'll be going to squeeze sympathy out of his brother, she supposes, or to bury his face in Sheba's fur. Remorse makes her heart go faster – it always surprises her, that voice out of her mouth – but she turns back to the words on the screen. He'll understand when he's older why what she does is important. Life and death don't mean anything when you're a kid.

She's nearly finished her email to the board when there's a thundering down the stairs. The sound of a small foot sliding on the last step.

'Get out,' Lalita roars, before the door can open. The boys don't listen, maybe they didn't hear. They're already tearstained by the time they crash into the sitting room. By the looks of it, they'd been crying for a while before she screamed at them.

'She's gone,' cries Archan, 'We've looked everywhere, she's got out.'

Their panic fills the room.

The Baby takes someone's phone off the table and throws open the garden doors. 'Sheba,' he calls, 'SHEBA!' and shines the phone torch into every corner of the garden. It's dark now, of course. When did it get dark? They can hear him scream 'Sheba' from the other side of the broken-down blue shed, and then he's back in the living room, flushed, desperate.

Lalita swears and puts down the iPad. 'Stupid dog. She'll be in this house somewhere.'

They search it top to bottom. Loft, boys' room, front room. Archan pushes open what's left of the door to the master bedroom and scans the corners. Lalita goes into the garden to poke more thoroughly through the border of scrub and pampas. They search it again, and again, with increasing hopelessness, until Archan says what they already know. 'She's got out.'

'When was the door open? Who left the fucking door open?'

'I haven't seen her since yesterday.'

Lalita says they'll split up and cover the closer streets. It's all beating in her heart very quickly – the email, the awful thing on the boys' faces, a knot inside her from having got so angry and another knot from it being true, that they hadn't seen the dog all day and she'd not even realised. The night's warm; street-lights turn the pavement brown. Usually Archan's too anxious to go out in the dark by himself, but he braves it for Sheba, insisting that he'll check round the backroads. People's front rooms glow against blue brick as he passes, sneakers slapping, before he disappears into a cul-de-sac.

Lalita holds the Baby's hand and they head towards the river. They follow the route Sheba normally takes when they walk her: all the way down to the bank and then right until the lock. The path's deserted and barely lit. Trees loom bluely out of the dim; water makes sucking sounds under the jetty by the boat-house, lapping at the rotted spaces between planks. They shout

Sheba's name every minute. In between, the little boy lists all the things that he thinks might have happened to Sheba. Drowned. Hit by a car. Foxes. ('She's a big dog, but I don't think she could win a battle against a fox.') They go all the way to the next lock. If she's gone further than that, she's lost.

'Maybe Archan's already found her?'

But as soon as they get near the house again they can hear him calling out for her. He runs up when he sees them.

'She's gone,' he says, crying. 'She's dead. I know she's dead.'

The Baby starts crying too. 'Why did we think we could look after a dog?'

Those are someone else's words, Lalita knows. Their father has accused her more than once of adopting Sheba to entice the boys into spending more time with her. She stops behind them, listens out for a whine or a whimper one last time before they go inside.

Inside, she paces the halls like a weary general. 'No dog, obviously. It's okay. Tomorrow, we'll call the police. We'll put out signs. She's a very brave dog, Sheba. She's a guard dog.' She makes the signal to Archan that means, *Take over, I need a cigarette*.

When Lalita comes back inside, Archan is searching up the website of the local control society.

'It's no use,' she says, resettling in the nursing chair. 'Everyone in this town hates her. They'd all be happy to have her put down.' As she talks, she looks blankly ahead at the wall behind the couch. Sheba has made enemies in suburbia on account of a natural fierceness which has manifested as several bad habits – biting postmen; eating swans. They're militia dogs, originally. The insurgent army in Lalita's homeland use them to protect rebel bases.

'She's too fierce for these brunch-having boutique owners,' Lalita says to her son, still with that empty stare. 'She's strange to them, she frightens them, they want her dead. She's hot-blooded. And the swans provoke her—'

She's interrupted by her the sound of claws and the Baby rushing in, ecstatic. Sheba is lolloping after him with a silly smile. Archan jumps out of her chair, Lalita falls down in front of the dog bed; all three of them compete to heap love on Sheba, who wags her tail and pants, not understanding.

'I was brushing my teeth, looking out of the window and she was just outside. She was pushing her nose through the gate!' says the Baby.

Still on her knees, Lalita exhales, deep and shuddery. She looks up and her eyes are full of fire. 'It's a sign from God.'

3.

'What happened?'

Kolia doesn't have to search for clues in pockets or hunt down broken crockery in order to reverse-engineer a crime scene this time. Her grandmother's room has been busted open and torn apart, there's dismantled furniture all over the landing, and the front room's being used to showcase a smeared-out desktop painting which might at one point have depicted a bird bleeding to death.

(Archan hasn't decided whether he'll repaint the table, but he did scrub out the design that was there. It had been too sad and naked-looking to leave it finished like that, smelling of paint, unvarnished and rejected.)

Lalita had only looked puzzled at the suggestion that something might be up. So, Kolia's in the dichondra room, pulling up a chair across from the boys, interview-style.

'What happened?' she asks again.

'Mum's clearing out Ammama's room,' says Archan. 'She's doing up the house.'

'Why's it such a mess?'

'I think it was something to do with the dust.' He shrugs.

'We lost Sheba,' adds the Baby. 'But then we found her.'

Kolia nods. 'Okay, cool. And what happened the other day, when you texted me? You said you'd had a fight with Mum?

That you thought she wasn't well? I came round the next day to check on you.'

'We were at Dad's.'

'Because you weren't getting on with Mum?'

'Kind of,' says Archan. 'She said she was going to turn the internet off.'

'Right. And then you had a fight?'

He nods. 'But it's okay, we're friends now.'

'Why did your text say she threw a cup at you? I looked in the kitchen and it's still there.'

'She did.'

'No, I looked. Your *Death Note* mug's in the cupboard.'

He looks annoyed. 'My other favourite cup.'

Kolia sighs. 'Okay. Do you want me to talk to her?'

They both shake their heads no, immediately. 'We're fine now,' Archan says again.

'She's going to take us to Mauritius,' says the Baby.

Kolia ducks into the first-floor bathroom before she goes back downstairs. She flips the toilet lid closed and sits there for a while, until her sit bones start to hurt. She thinks, slightly covetously, of the red leather toilet seat in Wales. Then she crosses over to the bathroom cabinet.

This had been the holy grail when she'd been a preteen living here. Muddled ranks of creams and perfumes, lotions with bewildering active ingredients, lipsticks, balms, tints and scrubs – all with caps missing or satiny leaks, tiny tear-shaped globules hardened into paste. Kolia could swear some of these exact bottles were in this cabinet the first time round, never mind that that was more than a decade and two tenancies ago. In some places, this house is totally estranged from the house in which she grew up. In others, it's been almost perfectly reconstructed – a full-scale museum diorama of a previous life. There's a cube-shaped box on the bathroom counter, for holding make-up or jewellery. Five of its six identical sides are mirrored and the bottom of the cube is black and velvety, with the remains of a price tag still on. It had been in the bathroom the first time round. Kolia opens it: two pound coins and a stick of kohl, worn to the nub. She closes it again. The mirrored box always used to feel like the very essence of Lalita: shiny, glamorous, filled with expensive hotel samples. When she was fourteen, Kolia had sat naked on the bathroom tiles and used it to examine herself for the first time.

She puts the box back on the counter, draws the warm bathroom sense of standstill over her for a few more seconds before she goes back downstairs.

'Well?' says Lalita, smiling widely from the colonial couch. 'Did the boys pass their interview?'

Kolia sits opposite her. 'They said you did throw a cup. And that you're taking them to Mauritius?'

'That's true. Mauritius, I mean. I want to tell you about it later, when I have all the details. I know how you like things all planned out. But it's going to be so fun.' One of her legs is tense, extended. She taps her foot without stopping. Sheba, who's curled up next to Lalita's feet, looks perturbed. 'The cup thing, obviously, is just ridiculous. He's really in his lying phase at the moment. It's something to do with his anxiety, I think – he just tells people what they want to hear. Which means, just, lies and lies. You remember what his father was like, don't you? Men in general – God, my chambers at the moment . . .' She pauses – her foot quivers, then resumes. 'Anyway. Kolia, tell me about you, please. I feel like I don't know anything about your life at the moment.'

Kolia blinks at the sight of her mother leaning forward to listen, expansive and curious. The part of her that rolls over at attention clocks in; the SCOPP hums and twinkles.

'Oh, well,' says Kolia. 'There's not that much going on.'

'Have you thought more about what you're going to do? Generally, I mean? You can't teach those awful posh kids for the rest of your life. Not my daughter.' She laughs. 'It's like, the opposite of affirmative action.'

Kolia leans back in her chair, tucks her fingers into her palm. 'To be honest, I was thinking of actually going to the school. Helping Ammama out.'

Because of course, this is it, this is her purpose, the holy telos missing from all the Shoreditch parties! And every time she's felt anger towards her mother for saving this life or that life, for being a jazz singer, for being a classical dancer, it's been because until now, Kolia hasn't had her own meaningful experiences!

She looks up out of her vision at her mother sitting on the couch. Her hero mother, whose expression is suddenly so awful, so sad.

Lalita's foot is still going at a hundred miles an hour, she's wound up, she clutches the skin at her arm and twists it. But when she speaks, it's dirge-like, liturgical.

'It's good, I think. Like a really funny film. The Charmed Lives of Orphans.'

'What do you mean?'

'Well, think how it looks. Amma abandons me for those kids. You go away, move countries for them. They must be the luckiest orphans in the world.'

'You don't think it's a good idea?'

'No, of course it's a good thing. Because you're typically motivated by goodness, right? It's just ironic, I think, that you're leaving me to go and help out someone else who has recently bailed on me, at a time of medical crisis.'

'Ammama hasn't left you,' Kolia protests. 'You're literally living in her house.'

'Right, which will go to the Orphans.'

'She's giving it to you for now.'

'This house is falling down, you know, and I can't get anything for repairs or upkeep. Why? Because all the family money is going to that school. Hey, I guess at least you'll be able to get hold of some of it.' She bares her teeth in the mean, sharp smile that used to make Kolia run away crying. 'Maybe you could give me some pocket money. That would be nice.'

'You're fifty-six. You have a job,' says Kolia, trying not to shout. 'The house is falling down because of you, by the way, because you're tearing it up. Get the window fixed. Stop ripping doors off their hinges.'

'I have a job, which pays like shit, because I am saving lives. This has always been an issue with you – you've always hated that I can't give you money like your father can—'

'Right now you're jealous of orphans, Mum.'

'It's not about the Orphans. Why do you side with my enemies? You always have, always. Ammama. Social Services. Your father.' She does the mean, sharp smile again. It transforms her whole face into something alien, something carnivorous and hateful. She's still smiling when she says, 'Did you know your dad hit me?'

'No, he didn't,' says Kolia immediately.

'Actually' – she makes a face like she's thinking back in time – 'he hit me while I was pregnant with you.'

'Shut up.' Kolia gets out of the chair, her voice rising wildly high. 'You're a liar. You're going to get disbarred. You don't even have gallstones.'

'Is that what your dad says?'

Kolia backs out the room. 'You always do it like this. You fuck up anyone that tries to help you. You suck them in and then chase them off. And you're doing it again because I'm obviously never coming back now.' And she turns and storms away, from the house that's falling down and the woman falling down in it.

The hedges flash up at her, green and at eye level. They start and stop in even paint-strokes as she runs down the road. Mostly, they have two functions. They're decorative, as befits any badge or facade or first point of contact with the world, and they stop passers-by from looking in. Two functions: showing and hiding.

4.

Gabriel joins Kolia and Mia at a park in Southwark a few days later. They sit on the grass, facing the river and drinking beer from cans. The Thames is wide and green under Tower Bridge, shallow in the heat; it breaks against the bank in listless slaps. They're an hour downriver from the stretch by the grey weir where Lalita had tried to drown.

Kolia isn't trying to assemble the troops. She doesn't want to talk them through her last conversation with Lalita. Gabriel can't help her, because there's no way to bring it up to him without that old plaintive, relentless inflection sneaking into her voice. 'I'm having a hard time': groping towards attention, no different from 'Your dad hit me'.

And Mia can't help her, because she's dealing with her own problems at work.

She picks at the grass, loops a tufty blade under the edge of her nail, as if to floss for dirt; she avoids Kolia's eyes as she tells the story.

'I was in the middle of literally testing his son on spelling and he started asking me where I was from. He said I looked distinctive. That I had such a special bone structure. And when I told him, he got so excited, and then he goes, that's where our table's from! *Actually*, he says, that's where the wood's from, because originally, "over there", it had been a hospital bed. Their dinner table is a repurposed hospital bed. Like, put aside all the fetishy, exotifying overtones, and that's still just unsanitary.'

'That's vile.'

'And bad luck, surely. Dining with death.'

Mia shakes her head, as if to dislodge Theo's overfamiliar dad. 'You know the name of this park is the old name for a paupers' graveyard? We're probably sat drinking on top of a hundred unmarked graves. Graves for criminals and gays.'

Gabriel fact-checks on his phone, while Kolia thinks, *Before the nineteenth century, a suicide would be buried at a crossroads with a stake driven through their heart.*

'No, you goth,' he says. 'This one actually does just mean Potters Fields. Like, because there used to be so many potters here.'

'Ceramicists, not suicides,' says Kolia. 'Meaning Gabriel's mum, not mine.'

Mia smiles at last. She shakes the final drops out of her Heineken onto nobody's grave, crushes the can. The park is almost empty: an old man sits on a bench with his trolley; a teenage couple sunbathe, having surely skived off school. It seems vaguely funny that Kolia, Gabriel, Mia should all be free on a weekday afternoon – that none of them have proper jobs, only odd bits of work, undertaken in fits and starts. They're free agents, Kolia supposes. But they don't seem free, not even Gabriel, who gets to write nonsense rather than tutor variously nightmarish children. It's that absence of purpose again, that missing telos. Everyone wants to do something, really.

But they aren't real people yet, only background and stimuli. No core, no content stronger than context. It was a thought Kolia had over the weekend – she'd made something for the first time in ages, still wired from running away past all those flashing hedges. It was thinking of the hedges that had started it: of hiding under and behind them. And of an old lecture on the original wind-weathered frames of Edvard Munch, where she'd learned that the frame was a mother holding its child.

Kolia prefers the mount, which is neither frame nor art. Neither inside, nor outside: it separates the picture from the glass, the way a hedgerow softens the space between a house and its garden wall. It surrounds and it encloses; it provides protection and distance. Two functions: showing and hiding. Still avoiding Francesca's missed calls and the pomegranate pith in the wastebin, Kolia had gone to Snappy Snaps, where she'd picked up all kinds of mounts. Engraved, oval-cut, bevelled to prevent shadowing. The A2 mount that her dad had insisted on putting over her *Extraordinary Machine* poster; the tri-cut mounts that Mia's parents preferred; a shiny mount made of brown cardstock, which looked a little like the frame that the package tape made around her mother's broken window.

There was a blonde girl at the counter asking if the Snappy Snaps lab could go through her photos while they were developing and get rid of any pictures featuring a man with crazy black hair. ('Sorry for the trouble,' she'd said, 'I'm just trying to avoid any nasty surprises.') Kolia had free reign of the photocopier. She'd scanned the mounts in, printing an incrementally smaller copy each time. Each mount would frame a Xerox of itself, and each of those Xeroxes would frame another Xerox, until the final image was so faint that it was almost nothing. Being almost nothing, the final results hadn't cheered her very much at all, and she'd sent them away with a faint sense of hopelessness.

(Later, she spotted the photographs that had been thrown out. Three shocks of black hair in the small bin behind the Snappy Snaps counter, like knots pulled off a brush. The man was fully visible twice, once on a bench in a tiled garden and again smiling by a fountain, arm around the blonde. In the corner of another photo: a red cocktail and mountains. All of Kolia's clever, invisible Xeroxes seemed bloodless in comparison to the glow of that red cocktail.)

She had felt so strongly that teaching at her grandmother's school would be her deliverance – had felt it with urgency and momentum – before the argument with Lalita. Now all she feels is a nebulous sense of defeat. There's no reason she shouldn't still go. No reason but laziness, inertia; Heineken warm in the grass and Gabriel's hand on her thigh.

His hand's on her thigh but he's facing both of them, opening his mouth to show them the wisdom tooth that's got stuck coming in. He's really opening up: the corners of his lips are straining and Mia shoots Kolia a look like, *Is he okay?* She's reminded of the pink-grey roof of Enzo's mouth, the back moving filmily, the scream that sucked her inside it.

'Isn't it nice that you never really need to go to the dentist?' says Mia. 'Our gums are, like, superpowered. Every problem will take care of itself if you wait long enough.'

Kolia's phone lights up with one alert, then two. She makes a face at the messages before it occurs to her that making a face might be categorised as SCOPP behaviour. Too late.

'What's up? All good?'

'It's not your mum?'

It is, of course.

The first text had come that morning, after days of radio silence. It's Lalita's usual pattern. Silence conveys her shock and hurt; renewing contact conveys a new tactic. Once they start back up, the communication is usually made up of threats, expressions of self-loathing, or pleas for forgiveness. The texts today are unusual. There's the classic threadbare apology, a bid for reconciliation, both familiar. But mostly, the messages are about God.

Lalita's written something about the dog and the river, about a 'sign' before they'd fought. She's written to say that when Kolia stormed out, instead of getting angry or taking downers, she'd prayed for hours. She's been listening to meditations, she's been doing yoga. Over the course of this week, she's found herself in a better place than she's been in years. She hopes that Kolia comes back to witness her new state of mind first hand. She doesn't expect Kolia to believe it otherwise. It's hard to believe: it's a miracle.

The most recent text reads:

[16:19] It doesn't matter if you don't come back. Becoming more spiritual is helping me understand that I will be fine either way. So really, I want you to go and live your life and don't think about me.

Lalita isn't a stranger to faith. The gods have been a household presence for as long as Kolia can remember. They disguised themselves and fought each other and placed bets in her grandmother's stories; now they sit on a metal tray on top of the microwave. Lalita had taught her the traditions that she knew: they drew shapes in rice on the floor of each new home and there were a few months of Bharatanatyam classes in a Surbiton community centre but Kolia lost interest when it didn't come naturally. She had liked the little flood of gold chains that followed her first period but she still isn't sure what things are okay to pray for. Lalita had taken her to a temple in Wimbledon to pray for luck in her exams. Colourful plaster idols loomed in a stone foyer, and everyone was talking about a recent change in exam boards. It seemed then like a diluted, diasporic version of religion. Thames Hinduism: an ancient undertow, sometimes reassuring.

The next text brings her back to her senses, this end of the Thames.

[16:23] I'm practising non-attachment. I'm trying not to experience want. So I won't bother you any more.

'God,' says Mia, reading it. 'Non-attachment. She's going full Vedic.'

Kolia cracks her next beer open, trying to ignore that familiar fractiousness, which has surfaced at Mia saying 'full Vedic'. There'd been a brief period during which every friend she had seemed to be suddenly exploring their spiritual side: reading *Siddhartha*, getting into transcendental meditation, practising Ayurveda. Mostly it was done with thought and research, and sometimes it was interesting to hear about – one happy conversation about Om with Mia had elucidated something her grandmother had been trying to explain for years – something to do with the white light she'd told Kolia to gather around her body to ward off nightmares. Still, she'd been glad when the zeitgeist passed.

[16:27] Archan's having trouble with the new way of the house. Making space for God in his life. Of course, it's the anxiety, which makes him hate change. But I keep telling him he can't live like this.

The way some of her friends understood God was heavy on academia, light on feeling; almost the opposite of how her mother thinks about it. Lalita's more instinctive, inventing an approximation of the laws based on what felt right as much as dimly remembered teachings. And, doubly removed from the source (her grandparents, her grandparents' country), Kolia's understanding is even more approximate. She'd learned certain rules from Lalita. You couldn't touch a book with your foot. You couldn't put a bottle of alcohol on the same tray as the statues of the gods. You had to wash the statues, touch your hands to their feet and then to your head.

The rules implied other underlying truths. The statues were an extension of the gods and had to be treated with a kind of pure touch; some ways of being were clean and holy, and others were dirty and unsanctified. Growing up, Kolia refined the rules with guesswork. In some places, the guesswork solidified into an unbreakable system; for example, if she accidentally brushed past a pile of books and couldn't identify which one made contact with her ankle, every book was touched to her head, then to the brass feet of the nearest statue, then back to her head. These laws verged on the same kind of religious OCD that struck anorexia mirabilis into the hearts of fourteenth-century saints: no crumb pure enough to be permitted entry. In other places, the guesswork was murky and contradictory. She couldn't get into her pyjamas until she'd decided whether it was disrespectful to the statues to be naked in front of them, or whether it was natural, even pure, and she only had instinct and speculation to base the decision on. Once she would have said that this way of thinking implied a bone-deep spiritual understanding, preferable to book-learned doctrine. Now, on the rare occasion that those kind of theological conundrums present themselves – is it sinful to steal amphetamines under the eyes of the god statues? Will killing the spider in this public bathroom be bad for my karma? Can I have sex under this Ganesha postcard? – she can admit it feels more like reaching out in the dark.

Lalita's texts suggest more certainty than ever about her own understanding of God. It makes sense that hers is the first kind of understanding, the place where the guesswork has hardened

into steel wire. Six hundred years ago she'd have been self-flag-
ellating in a tower somewhere, swearing that she'd seen the
pietà cry blood. Today, she's limited to having personal epipha-
nies every twenty seconds.

[16:32] Feeling this spirituality is helping me be a better mother
to Archan, so you don't have to worry about him. I'm working
hard not to lose another child.

'She's a lunatic,' Kolia says aloud. She feels a little twinge,
which she attributes to Mia's habit the year before of correcting
anyone who used words like 'lunatic' or 'insane'. They were
ableist terms, Mia said, and disproportionately directed towards
women. Who decides where to draw the line between 'she's
crazy' and 'she's just too much'? (It's true that Archan's father
tried to get Lalita sectioned for changing her tampon on a train
platform.) Kolia's used to Mia being her conscience, though it
really grates when Gabriel contradicts her.

[16:38] Archan is going mad. I worry, because I see myself in
him. I know he needs God.

'What's she saying?'
'Archan's mad,' says Kolia. She doesn't want to go into God
right now with Mia, the euro-Buddhist.
'God, it's unreliable narrators on unreliable narrators.'
'He's not mad,' says Kolia, 'or unreliable. He's just anxious.'
He's very anxious, that's not one of Lalita's fabrications. She
likes to say that the anxiety's made him a liar, but he only
really seems to lie to get out of school. Gabriel turns his beer
upside down, starts telling them about an anxious cousin who
cured himself by micro-dosing shrooms. Kolia leans back,

opens her shoulders up towards the sun. She pictures Archan's small, flickering face. He has their mother's sharp nose. She inhales, exhales.

It used to be a compliment, inheriting tendencies from Lalita. ('Your mother's eyes!') It used to be a coup. Lalita had bought a doll's house for Kolia's eighth birthday, a locket on a chain for her ninth. 'I knew you'd like them,' she'd said, 'because that's what I always wanted when I was your age.' The power there – the joy in Lalita saying, 'That's what I was like at your age.' Now, inheritance only means pathology. Inherited madness, inherited horror. No, there's nothing of that in Archan; he's anxious, that's all. And there's nothing in Kolia, really. It's been years since she set the little fires in the alley at the side of her house.

Look at her, a friend and a lover, sat in a London park, receiving these texts without flinching, staunch like a rock in a river. The Thames moves again and again in the same way over the same bit of curved rock like something in a factory.

5.

It's late when they leave. Mia goes home first; Kolia has another drink with Gabriel. He pulls her hair when they kiss, too close to the scalp, and then has to run for a bus. Darkening sky, still hot. Half an hour walk from Potters Fields towards Waterloo.

She passes the docks, thinking of Virginia, who wrote how dockside at Tower Bridge the city suddenly thickens, the buildings 'heap themselves higher'; Virginia, who drowned herself, of course, by walking into a river with stones in her pockets. Everything seems laminated this side of the bridge: built up, paved with shiny squares, reflecting the heat back. She heads past, onto older stone, and the air's suddenly cooler, more pleasant. A cormorant struggles with a big fish, tossing it up and catching it repeatedly, trying to find the perfect angle. The moment shines: waxy black feathers, gleaming scale. Kolia watches blankly, knowing it's funny, trying to feel it.

Walking down the South Bank, her right eye starts getting tired. At first she thinks it's that her riverside eye's working overtime to keep up with the constant flux of the water, compared to the more solid bustle of the landscape on her left side. Then she thinks that this is it, her gentle myopia kicking in for real, amping up, her eyes are failing. She tries to unthink this as soon as it occurs to her, defending against an instinctive suspicion that thinking of illness will make her ill. Something to do with

sending the bad thought straight to the cell; a science proven by
the fact that if she even thinks about getting a spot, one appears.
It's not a reasoned theory, she knows, but it still frightens her.
Magnetic thoughts; power in the electrical impulse. The same
superstition means if she thinks something awful, the gods will
know – but only if she thinks it in the same room as their statues.
Her own short-sightedness is suddenly overwhelming. Kolia's
brain has stopped filling in the gaps and now all that remains are
their smudgy prompts. People approach her and she cannot see
their faces, cannot read their intention until they're too close, it's
too late, they pass her with a sliver of space between them. She
stops in her tracks, holds on to a wall. She looks down over the
side, waiting for her eyes to adjust. For a second, a shallow under-
lit fountain rushes up at her – the ground floor from the shopping centre in her mother's town, the falling woman's view. Kolia
blinks. The Thames reasserts itself.

A non-decomposable lei of plastic cherry blossom washes
towards the pier, a neon ghost of the mythic belt in Sicily. A
little boat catches Kolia's eye, blue, battered. A pleasure cruiser.
The lei-tossing culprit, she thinks, eyeing the passengers.
They're dancing on the tiny deck. One of the passengers has
fresh stitches in his hand, deep and thick enough that she can
see them, even short-sighted, even from ashore. He's maybe
thirty, the guy with the stitches: muscular, one protective bicep
curled around his girlfriend, but moving his hips with a femi-
nine looseness. Kolia glances over at the man at the wheel. The
only non-dancer, he's looking straight ahead, skin tight from
years of exposure. She recognises him. Surely not. How could
she know? But she's fixed by the certainty that he's the captain
from her grandfather's funeral. That whole morning recalls
itself in an instant: Kolia, fifteen, looking from the fat priest to
the racing kayaks. She leans over the embankment railings,

looking for the name – *Meriadoc*. But it must be on the other side of the boat.

She watches them for a while, until a sudden freshness in the air marks the sun going in.

On the train home from Waterloo, Kolia makes eye contact with a cyclist in an orange safety vest. She realises she's been staring and looks down, contrite, takes out her phone.

[19:04] think if he has cleaner life in the village where actually getting back to people will make him happy. And he doesn't realise it's about being happy. He thinks it's just about a forensic thing of school and work. So have booked flight for tomorrow morning.

[19:06] really nice boarding school at this one he will go out swimming in the lakes and fishing in the paddy fields that I used to go in when I was a girl and it is the east and it is so fundamentally different and so external that he won't be in a position where he's in his head, which is always the problem, I know what it's like to feel really safe by snuggling on the duvet and just ignoring everything, and I really believe that he's going to come back fundamentally changed.

[19:06] he can start immediately because problem case and ammama will pick him up at station.

The train goes into a tunnel just as Kolia starts reading the bit about lakes and paddy fields. By the time it surfaces, she's already dialled her mother's number. Voicemail immediately. Kolia swears, calls again. She calls and calls the whole way home, to no response. The cyclist in orange is avoiding her gaze.

*

The next morning it's confirmed. Archan's on the plane. He's gone. Lalita forwards her an acceptance email from a vaguely fancy boarding school in the south of the island country, a Hogwarts with mosquito nets and tennis courts. Could this still, somehow, be a trick? The occasional entertainment value of Lalita's lunacy is in the bin. In the end, Ammama's the one to verify the claim. Even once he lands, Archan won't have the roaming data to reply to Kolia's messages.

Kolia remembers when Archan was born, the way she used to always dream about him getting lost or kidnapped or shrunk into a tiny floating bubble from which he could not escape and how she always woke up just before she could save him.

This time she's going to get him.

PART 5: ROAD TRIP

Some things happen slowly and some things all at once. Archan's flight, for example, took nearly a whole day. He'd watched four different films on the seatback touchscreen, and every time he paused to switch over to the Current Journey display, the pixel plane had barely moved. He watched *Forrest Gump* from beginning to end without leaving Iranian airspace! But then everything afterwards was one unbroken rush: Ammama on the other side of baggage reclaim; her driver, who'd brought her all the way from the village in a car that smelled too strongly of petrol, as if something had leaked; the sudden white surge of The British School; its principal, strikingly English, his hands on Archan's shoulders as if to confirm the handover; a dorm, with a narrow bed which they called a cot; all at once nobody around – the sound of football in a glimpsed courtyard – someone would be by to show him to lunch.

Archan stares at the dormitory walls. They're white and slightly curved, like the inside of an empty eggshell. An insect whines from somewhere behind him. He thinks of Gary Sinise with confetti in his hair.

1.

'I want to get a jumper,' says Mia. 'It's always so cold once you're in the sky.'

She leads them through half the stores in the departure lounge, her suitcase jerking around its one busted wheel. ('Why do airports only have the most random shops?')

Kolia stops herself frowning. The fractious, tight-shouldered child in her might wish that Mia would take the whole thing more seriously, but she's still Kolia's single symbolic defence against being totally dependent on the old lady saint.

They've bypassed her mother entirely, of course; she's not sure whether or not Ammama might relay the rescue plans to Lalita, but she suspects not. Nowadays Ammama barely seems to process information that doesn't concern the Orphans. That's the reason Kolia's here, in the Heathrow Ted Baker: Ammama's agreed to pay for both their flights on the understanding that they'll start their journey with a visit to her school first. It's not ideal. They'll lose at least a day and a night on their dutiful tour and then it's an eight-hour drive to the boarding school, which is at the other end of the country. Kolia pictures Archan silent, crying in a school toilet, and the rage flares back up: at Lalita for sending him there; at Ammama. for not seeing the urgency of retrieving him. Ammama probably thinks the sight of all the tiny orphaned faces will stun Kolia into signing up to volunteer there permanently. She doesn't know that Kolia's already arrived at that decision, that her epiphany about purpose and do-gooding has already happened, tucked between Gabriel's grey sheets. Kolia doesn't need visual evidence.

Although, of course, the wind has already been taken out of her sails a little, epiphany-wise. She'd spoken to her dad on the train up, and he'd talked her down even further. It had been an early start, and black outside; it's probably still dark now, though Kolia can't tell from inside the airport. They hadn't slept at all, just paced Mia's kitchen, making circles around their luggage. The coffee at the station tasted like toothpaste. She'd called her father once the train had departed. Not to discuss the rescue or anything Lalita had told her, just to hear his serious, methodical voice, the voice of the man who'd cried at the swans. He'd picked up after one ring.

They talked peaceably. He doesn't like it when she calls him from the train; he objects to the background noise and disturbing the peace of other passengers and Kolia being less aware of her surroundings. But if he heard the tannoy in the background he didn't say anything. When he asked why she was calling, Kolia said that she was thinking of going to work at Ammama's school.

'What do you think?'

There'd been a long pause. When he spoke, it was surgically precise.

'I think it's a terrible idea. There's no doubt in my mind that your grandmother's school will be fundamentally mismanaged. It's running on, basically, the machinery of good intentions. She's a serially delusional woman, who was married at sixteen, never educated beyond that, has never run a business or an institution before, and has suddenly made herself responsible for hundreds of children. She will be easy to take advantage of, because people who believe that they have a higher calling are easy to take advantage of, as are people who believe in God. I think there will be staff on her payroll who are exploiting her, people in the village presenting themselves as charity cases who are exploiting her. I don't think she'll have any idea of how to structure a curriculum. From what I gather, most of her teachers are volunteers with little to no background in education, many of whom do not speak the native language. If you were to start work there, you would be a volunteer with little formal background in school teaching who can't speak the language. Your grandmother's not unlike your mother, in terms of inability to handle administration, lack of attention to detail, all those bureaucratic skills that are necessary for something to operate. This feeling that she has, of being "destined" to help, is very, very far removed from an ability to execute. I wouldn't be surprised if it's been misregistered as a charity or if there turns out to be some kind of bamboozling relating to charitable contributions, whether or not your grandmother's aware of it. I think, most likely, it's a car crash of an institution in a country that's still on fire and that you should stay a million miles away from it.'

Her father goes on these lengthy, eloquent spiels all the time, usually when they're discussing her mother, so Kolia wasn't sure why this one had hit her like cold water. It was surprisingly upsetting to hear. Especially the way he'd said 'married at sixteen'. And 'people who believe in God'.

Ammama's black-toothed primordial force had deflated at his words. Kolia hasn't inherited purpose or deep-seated, Shakti-rooted power; she's not inherited anything but good intentions. (For a second she'd really believed that Ammama's skin was so good because she looked after God's children.) Kolia could remember a holiday, Portugal, back when her parents were still married. There was a crack in the plaster of the rented villa and

Ammama had spent an hour laying splinters of Pringle out, cooing at the ants which marched out of the crack to retrieve the bounty and march it back. Kolia had thought her grand-mother was like an old lady saint then, before she'd seen her dad's expression underneath his sunglasses.

His voice on the phone carried her all the way to Heathrow. They both said, 'Bye, love you,' as though he hadn't just spent half an hour tearing her idea apart. Kolia suspects it happens because he lives alone and, apart from talking to her, most of his interpersonal communication takes place in lecture theatres. He doesn't know how to speak normally any more: his neutral cadence is uninterruptable, declamatory academia. Sometimes when she's angry, Kolia imagines him as one of those Cyclopses that live in cave systems, ranting and going mad. She pictures him wandering about her childhood home with all the rooms filled with shallow water, making coffee and talking to himself, voice rising interminably, stony with sobering practicalities. He's so different in manner from Lalita, who mostly talks nonsense but with an enthusiasm that makes gold from thin air. When Kolia was young, she'd felt prepared for the future by Lalita's oversharing – dizzying forthrightness on abortions and orgasms. And by the manic sincerity with which she would call Kolia the most beautiful girl in the world.

His solitariness upsets her sometimes. His solitariness and his sparse, surprised-looking eyebrows, the beginnings of a crook-edness in his shoulders which no amount of Phileas Fogg deportment can hide. Kolia remembers the last book she read: the protagonist's age was never given exactly but she'd never wondered, because his father had died in the opening scene and so she knew that he was father-dying age. If anything does happen to Kolia's dad, there's no one to help him but her. Her turn to unball the socks in the laundry basket; her life locked back up in that town with its towpaths and bandstands and no way out. (She thinks of Ammama's hands twitching over the handles of a suitcase.)

She'd put her phone away.

'What's he saying?' Mia had asked, raising her head sleepily from Kolia's shoulder.

'He's saying stay away. That Ammama's just like Mum and nothing good comes from letting them draw me in. And he's right. I mean, this kind of stuff only happens when I'm on speaking terms with my mother.'

'What kind of stuff? Cool stuff? Adventure stuff? Rescue-mission road trip stuff?'

(Mia does that all the time. Whatever lunacy Kolia's mother claws her into, Mia will comedise, minimise; she's unusually predisposed to taking Lalita's side. *What are you, team H&M?* Maybe that's what Kolia's looking for: someone with enough sympathy for Lalita to counteract the unnatural, treacherous deviancy of a child saying such awful things about her mother in the first place.)

Mia is no longer looking at jumpers for the flight; she's found an eye mask, pink satin, holds it up for Kolia's approval. The words *Beauty Sleep* are embroidered in cursive sequins. It's funny for a second, then not at all. Kolia feels a premonition, cold going up her spine, that this is the kind of levity that invites ruin. The slip of pink satin seems already tragic, like the only thing that would be found whole in the wreckage of a plane crash.

2.

The plane doesn't crash. They land in the evening, at a tin-can of an airport, small enough that they can see the whole building as soon as they get off the plane. The sun's just starting to go down. It doesn't feel right that the island's only five and a half hours ahead of London. It's always seemed so remote to Kolia, as if the time difference might be days.

They wait out front for Ammama's driver, stripping down to their T-shirts in the dry heat.

'A driver,' says Mia. She rotates her suitcase on the bad wheel, like a dancer on pointe. 'Does your grandma have servants?'

'I'm not sure,' Kolia says, truthfully. 'Ammama always makes it sound like people in the village just . . . do stuff for her. To say thank you, because they like her, and for the school and stuff. But it might be more along the lines of Lalita getting her trainees to babysit, like it's a fair trade. Or a privilege, even.'

She thinks of the Kurdish intern, the one who'd sometimes dressed as an elf, and who'd saved her from being touched by grown men; she zones out and then in, feeling bad that she's not focused on absorbing this, these first precious minutes in the land of her forebears. There's not much to absorb – the wide, unbusy road, the airport's name mown in balding letters on a short lawn – until suddenly the car shows up, rattly, peeling blue.

The driver hands Kolia a flip-phone through which she can just hear Ammama, crackling and faraway, explain that he doesn't speak English. He loads their bags; Ammama says something indecipherable and hangs up. Inside the car, there's such a strong smell of fuel that Mia stops breathing in, and Kolia, committed now to absorbing, absorbs that there are no seatbelts or suspension. They wind the windows all the way down and stick their heads out. It's not rude, Kolia thinks, since they've established the impossibility of conversation.

It's an hour's drive. At the beginning, so much is strange and delightful. Pink plaster bus stations. A shallow grey lake that looks at risk of evaporating at any second. The light in it! A few small breezeblock houses; one, candy-coloured, with a shrine in the front garden bigger than the house itself. When they pass the first road block, both girls turn to make sure the other has seen it. A handful of uniformed men, cigarettes, sunglasses and long black guns, a sign promoting 'unity in diversity' written in three languages. (Kolia, still absorbing, remembers helping her mother type up medical testimony: discoloration as a result of being beaten with an officer's riflebutt.) The stretch afterwards is quiet, pleasant, the sudden grandness of a restaurant with nothing but fields either side. Notice of a war memorial and then: an unmanned guard hut, a far-off crimson stone. There's a busier distance for a while – lusher growth, a few bigger houses, a single-storey assembly hall – and then this tapers off into nothing but green, a tealight burning in a roadside shrine. The evening's settling, cooling. It's still warm enough to be naked, but the scorch has been taken out of it.

A second roadblock. (Again Kolia thinks of beatings, government officials and their gunstocks. Black-and-white photographs of bruising.) Afterwards, the land around them draws into a thin spout until it becomes apparent they're at the exit of a peninsula, and then suddenly they're rattling down a thin neck of road, blue sea on either side.

'I think we're about halfway there,' she says confidently, once the strip of road has rewidened into mainland. She's not certain. She's only seen the shape of this country in pixel and on paper. It wasn't like this, cranes and junk heaps and the faint, almost imaginary smell of warm kelp. All at once – a white salt flat, in sudden thin stretches like snow.

This side of the bridge is even less built-up. Nothing but green for fifteen minutes, cow-grazing and rice paddies. When that passes: stone buildings, skeletons of shacks. She knows what this is. This is where the worst of the fighting took place, towards the end of the war. You can spot these areas easily: they appear as sudden clearings. The tall, dense vegetation disappears and everything is suddenly flat and open. You can tell them by the palm trees alone, few and short, almost comically stubby – more knobs than trees; none of them older than ten years. The government called these safe zones, decreed that anyone outside of them would be considered an insurgent. They marshalled civilians here, and then began to systematically kill them. Tens of thousands dead.

Kolia sits back in her seat, rolls the window up. She watches the back of the driver's head for a while, torn between relief at not being able to speak the language and wishing she could say anything at all. The car clatters down a last, long side road in silence, and then they've arrived.

The driver stays with the car; another man is waiting to take their luggage. He's thin and tall, somewhere in his twenties, dark circles under his eyes like a brown Tim Burton character. Kolia's fairly sure he's a relative.

'That's the school,' he says, pointing towards an iron gate on their left. They can't see anything over the top. He leads them across the road to an identical iron gate. 'This is the house,' he says, and unlocks it.

The yard is yellow and green: tall palms, a few shorter mango trees. Mia freezes when she first spots the four or five stray dogs and gives them a wide berth, though they seem slow from the sun and unbothered, almost lifeless. The house is a single-storey complex, the colour of terracotta. Ammama's waiting at the door.

Kolia holds her tight, is momentarily bulwarked by the padded weight of her. Ammama lets herself be hugged. When Kolia pulls away, her grandmother treats her to the same serene, dispassionate smile with which she greets Mia and the Tim Burton man. She looks different here. It's not just that she's not wearing velour: her face is shining more clearly than ever.

'Janaka, take the bags,' she says, and Tim Burton disappears. 'Okay, come.'

They follow her into the house, which is full of the noise of the ceiling fan, and lit with citronella candles.

'You'll sleep here.'

'It's a beautiful home,' offers Mia politely.

'Who lives here?'

'Me. Nila, who teaches. Gayathri, one of our students. I'm taking her in for now. Her dad is hitting her. Her mum won't stop going back to him. Janaka stays with us, in an annexe, for security.'

Kolia grimaces at Mia, a look that's supposed to say, *Sorry, this is just what it's like spending time with my family, nothing but horrible, sad news, all the time.* Mia, of course, is nodding sympathetically, eyes wide with pure understanding. Kolia drops the grimace and sits on the edge of the guest bed, feeling evil and tired.

Nila brings them black tea. They watch the palm trees turn into silhouettes through the insect screens. When the last light's gone, the frogs start calling out. A bird makes a ringtone sound in the dark.

'What bird is that?'

'The bird that lives in the lake.'

'There's a lake?'

'It's too late to explore. Go to sleep, girls. Tomorrow we'll get to the school nice and early.'

Kolia catches her grandmother's wrist before she can turn the lamp off. 'You dropped Archan off at the school, didn't you? How was he?'

'Fine,' says Ammama, short and sharp. She's been waiting for this question and wants it to be done with.

'You didn't think – you thought he'd be okay? Leaving him there?'

'It's a very good school,' says Ammama. 'Everyone knows it. International. All the teachers are from Europe or America – they've gone to Ivy Leagues. Very good.'

'Very good,' Kolia murmurs. 'How did he seem? He wasn't expecting it at all, you know.'

'He seemed fine. Tired, from the flight. Like you two.' She puts the lamp out and leaves.

The two of them lie there sightlessly. After a few minutes, Kolia hears Mia shuffling. Some clacking sounds.

'Literally, what are you doing.'

'Sorry,' Mia whispers, sounding like she's trying not to laugh. 'Trying to charge my phone. I can't see – but that was so intense and I didn't want to disrupt your thought process . . .'

Kolia shakes her head, even though Mia can't see her. She passes over the citronella candle, aglow in its jar, and waits until she can hear Mia guide the charger into place.

'Done, done, sorry. I'll be quiet now. Man.'

'I know,' says Kolia.

'How are you feeling?'

'I'm feeling like I'm very grateful that you're here.'

The night chorus purrs in the dark, frogs and crickets, the fan humming on its stem, even Mia's soft dreaming huffs. Beautiful sounds in the little room. In the dark, Kolia is approaching the boundaries of a feeling, something dim and blurry, but she falls asleep before she can name it.

3.

'Für Elise' rips through the house with the morning light. It's coming from somewhere outside, loud enough to travel another hundred miles: shrill, thin, plinky notes that place the song immediately among the Für Elises of piano apps or ringtone websites. Kolia bolts awake, sure that half the jungle must be shaking, high-Richter shudders in the damp, matted green.

That's the bun man, Janaka explains. He sells sugar buns out of his van. 'And . . .' Janaka holds up his finger so that they can hear the clatter and baying of the strays chasing after the vehicle. 'Like an alarm clock,' he says.

('I like Janaka,' Mia says, getting changed after breakfast. They've been given someone else's clothes to wear to the school; kurtas and loose pants, possibly Nila's.

'Me too,' says Kolia, but it isn't true. He rubs Kolia up the wrong way somehow, living with her grandmother and knowing all the sounds. She considers her reflection in the wardrobe door.

'You look really brown,' Mia says helpfully.

'Thanks. You too.'

'Literally. I thought I'd stick out more but everyone's so dark here. I never realised, I thought your mum was just, like, extra melanated.'

'Yeah, Lalita thinks we're a lost African tribe.'

'Hmm.'

'That's what I said.')

The heat is staggering by the time they leave the house. It's well past drop-off, but a few of the parents are talking outside, resting astride their Vespas. Their conversation dies when Mia and Kolia appear and Kolia feels very suddenly shy as she follows Janaka past, like she's crossing the road wrong, like it doesn't make sense for her to be here, slipping through the gates of her grandmother's school.

She has a moment's impression: a yard with swings and a ping-pong table; classrooms built at intervals with cement floors but no walls; dozens of heads turning away from a whiteboard; a yellow flowering tree and a stray dog underneath, biting itself. Then she's following Janaka again, slipping off her sandals at the door of Ammama's office. The office is more like a room than any of the classrooms – there are walls and windows, and a fan.

The fan is clearly intended to benefit Ammama, who sits at her desk in front of it. Without getting up, she introduces them to Nila and another teacher, who wave from the dimmer, warmer back of the office. On the shelf behind her is a photograph of Kolia's grandfather with thick hair and seventies aviators, propped up in between a calendar with a Saraswati illustration and a drawing one of the students must have done. And, next to it, Kolia's surprised to see a picture of herself, six or maybe seven years old, a photo she doesn't recognise. Wide, round face and eyebrows that meet in the middle.

'How cute,' says Mia.

'First grandchild,' says Ammama. 'You two will watch Janaka's lesson, okay? Then maybe, if you want, you can teach.' She doesn't wait for a nod, just squeezes out from behind her desk and gestures for the three of them to follow, turning the fan off behind her.

She takes them over to one of the outdoor classrooms, where a middle-aged woman in a pink sari is writing out the alphabet for a small group of six-year-olds. As soon as it becomes apparent that Ammama has elected to stop by their class, the game's up.

'Ma'am!' they screech delightedly, and flock to her like iron filings until she's disappeared from the waist down. Ammama smiles her beatific smile. She looks down at her adoring mob and speaks to them, a sing-song speechifying that sounds like the rhythm of her old stories about foxes and rivers.

'What's she saying?' Kolia whispers to Janaka.

'She's just telling them to work hard,' he says, 'so that they can honour God and the school.'

'The teacher's loving it,' says Mia, and it's true, the woman in the pink sari looks rapt, whiteboard marker going dry at her side.

A handbell rings from the office. Ammama's tiny fan club disperses; Ammama herself begins heading back into the cool. Janaka nods to them and replaces the woman at the board, wipes away her sigils. The students, who'd numbered under a hundred when they were all sat down, seem to suddenly multiply as they rush to the right place. Kolia watches them shout and hurry. She wonders briefly which of them is the boy with shrapnel in his head, the one who'd been reading *Artemis Fowl*, but is distracted by how many resemble her brothers in one aspect or another. A boy with Archan's nose brings them plastic folding chairs, bowing. Kolia bows back. The kids gathering on benches for Janaka's lesson must be around sixteen. He hands out battered copies of *Puss in Boots*.

The first girl called to read is painfully shy. She stands in front of the board and twists from side to side, speaking in whispers. The boy who reads next can't get a word out without hooting laughter from the girls' side of the benches. But Janaka is firm and patient and it gets better from there, although the fifth time that he tries to define 'Marquis of Carabas', Kolia thinks they really should have chosen a different book. They must have been a donation, the *Pusses*.

Lunch is served out of a small outbuilding of fogged glass. Janaka shows them to a balding hill in the corner of the yard where they eat rice and dhal and green bean curry with their hands. From the hill, which is about the height of a man, they can see over to the lake on the other side of the school wall. They watch someone cast a fishing line out from an outrigger boat some way in the distance; then they turn back around and watch the games of table tennis.

'You'll teach later?' Janaka asks them.

'Maybe.'

'I don't think so,' says Kolia. 'I don't think I can teach without speaking any of the language. It feels very presumptuous.'

'Teach English.'

'It's okay.' Kolia smiles tightly. 'I'll learn for next time.'

'I'm learning the language too,' says Janaka. 'That's why I only teach English now. But soon I could teach IT.'

'Oh,' says Kolia. 'I thought . . .' She's not sure how offensive Janaka might find her assumption that he was not only of her family's background, but actually of her family. 'But you understand everything my grandmother was saying.'

He's been learning for some time now, he explains, but he grew up in the south, on the other side of the war. He came here to study herpetology, before he heard about the school.

'There's a remarkable range of snake fauna that's gone unstudied because of the civil war. So many habitat types, both sides of the bridge. Coastal beaches at Maruthankerni; grass-lands at Karaveddai; mangroves at Elluthumaduval; monocul-ture plantations at Delft Island; salt marshes at Kayts. Road verges, scrub forests, natural inland water bodies. Artificial inland water bodies at Aliavalai and waste disposal sites at Valikamam and Elluthumaduval.'

Breathless singing from a clutch of girls by the swings. The jet lag and their hoarse, childish voices disorientate Kolia, send her spinning through the litany of snake places. She looks at her watch, which is still set to British Summer Time, as though it might draw her back out.

'But your grandmother's brother was teaching me English. And I was living with him, and I heard about the school,' Janaka is saying. 'And everything I'd learned since being in the north – I wanted to help. It's so good, this school. The children in this area had nothing like it. I spend all my time here now; I do nothing with snakes any more.'

The next lesson they shadow is a real downgrade. Some TEFL grad student crackling out of a laptop at a classroom of bemused eight-year-olds. It's clear that the school doesn't quite run smoothly. Kolia wonders about the gaps – the twenty minutes where it's not clear who should be taking the class, the impro-vised lesson contents, the bootlegged worksheets. How much can be put down to resource scarcity and lack of staff, and how much is the fundamental mismanagement that her father had described? Bureaucracy getting in the way of holy telos, just like Lalita's fiery purpose and her inability to bill her clients.

'Look.' Mia nudges her, points out a kid losing focus in the back row. 'Headfooters.'

The boy's drawing them in the back of his exercise book: tadpole people with legs coming straight out of their outsized faces. These should go on all the funding brochures. Misshapen, doodled proof that children are the same everywhere.

Even when he flips to another page (Kolia suspects he's showing off), every drawing appears as an old friend. It must be some psychic land that all children, and only children, occupy, this world that always has the sun in the corner of the page; the world of the triangle boat and the crescent moon, the triangle pyramids and the two-armed cactus. How funny: five thousand miles from Enzo, these kids also draw the square house and the scribble smoke. Though they must have other understandings of a house with smoke coming out.

Mia teaches the last twenty minutes, after the Zoom starts lagging for the dozenth time. She's good at it. She makes the children roar out the answers, tackling the biggest obstacle in their way of their spoken English, which is their shyness. They sing 'Bye, Miss' and 'Thank you, Miss' at the end, and one girl gives her an embarrassed hug.

'You were great,' says Kolia, back at the complex.

'Thank you.'

They sit in a hammock strung up between two of the mango trees. Halfway through pulling her legs up to cross them, Mia wobbles. She rarely looks ungainly, and it has the effect of making her seem instantly vulnerable, though only for the second it takes the hammock to settle.

'That girl hugged you,' says Kolia, slightly jealous.

'I know!'

'Did you see the boy who looked just like Archan?'

'I think so. With the really long lashes?'

'Yeah.'

Kolia rocks the hammock, dragging one foot in the dirt. The sky goes lilac, then dull. A flowery fading smell. 'I'm quite ready for us to be on our way,' she says.

The leaves fade down to spiky shapes. Above, the human laugh of a red macaw.

4.

Janaka will drive them south.

Mia nods understandingly. 'Did the other car break? We thought it might be leaking.'

'No,' Ammama says, frowning. An uncle in Colombo had done a charity drive; he had some textbooks for Janaka to bring back for the school. They had ten minutes for breakfast, string hoppers and Tetley, and if they weren't ready then, he'd be leaving without them.

Mia falls back asleep as soon as her seatbelt's on but Kolia's awake, her chest alive with nerves and earliness, though Janaka handles the car well. The roads are busier than they'd been on the way from the airport. Tuk-tuks and lorries, people riding on the back of trucks. A man in a sarong is selling rambutan at the junction. Vespas and fields and shrines, the bun man overtaking them with the sound of 'Für Elise' – and then another sudden length of short trees. She catches the dark-circled Scissorhands stare in the rearview mirror and looks away.

There are houses with no roofs and then, a little while later, roofs with no houses.

A while into the drive, Janaka pulls into a car park.

'I thought you might like to see this. Your grandmother stops here whenever she goes to Colombo.'

The temple is slight, hung with paper garlands, marked by the kind of neon sign you might find outside a London shisha bar. There are women singing by a flame. When Kolia goes closer, she can see that the temple has been built around an old tree trunk. A man sits on the ground by the trunk, with his prosthetic leg stretched out, a beggar or priest.

Janaka gets them sodas from a nearby stand.

'What are they doing?' she asks, gesturing at the women. It doesn't sound like the praying she's heard before.

'They're mourning. It's not allowed, actually. Last week was the birthday of the man who used to be in charge of the rebel militants. In the seventies. This week they say prayers for the dead. But if the soldiers see them, they'll be in trouble. People aren't really allowed to gather during this time, or wear flowers. The government destroyed the graves to prevent it, but they just come here instead.' He pauses. 'They make offerings for your grandmother here, and your mother.'

'My mother?'

'She's helped a lot of people. During the war, and after. They grind sandalwood for her.'

Kolia nods, not looking at Mia. She feels embarrassed and proud and guilty. A bit sick. She told Lalita she wouldn't see her. Again. She meant it. Pressure is building in a vein at the side of her skull, between her eye and her ear. She can sense the exact incision she could make to relieve the pressure. Can feel it – a stencilled cut, a phantom. The flame flickers in front of the tree trunk. One of the women goes to the altar, takes a waxy nub of camphor from a plate, holds it to the flame. It catches in seconds, and she drops it in front of the painted god of destruction. The way old cooks test the temperature with their hands, not flinching at the spat oil.

'You want to? You have to rinse your feet first.'

She washes her feet where Janaka tells her, with a kid's plastic bucket, and then circles back, past the singing women and the amputee, to stand in front of the god of luck. Kolia closes her eyes, sends meaning radiating out from her chest. Pride and guilt. The camphor catches quicker than she'd thought it would and fire suddenly licks, tall and bright, towards her arm.

'Shit,' she says, panicked, and throws it at the basket in front of the gods.

She's still groaning back in the car with her shoes on.

'Do you think that was bad luck?'

'I'm sure it wasn't,' says Mia.

'God. Let's go.'

She worries over the potential blasphemy as the car rattles on, over a road turning to red dust. War memorial, war memorial, pizza restaurant. She rubs her tired eyes; Janaka points out the junction of a famous battle.

'Do you just know everything? Do you know what kind of snakes there are here?'

'I make this journey a lot,' he says apologetically.

Kolia doesn't say anything else before she falls asleep.

She wakes up from a dream about Archan drowning in the bath at No. 25. She'd been trying to hold his head up but it wouldn't stop slipping out of her hands. She peers out of the car. It's darker now; it looks as if it's just rained. Shops and restaurants have the name of the city on their glowing signs. They must be driving through the capital.

Kolia thinks of this as the seat of the other side. North, where the Orphans' school and the complex and the macaws all are, is where her people, her mother's people are from. It's where their pearl-trading kingdoms once were. South is where the people who killed her people are, really. It's where the government and the administrative centres are, and the defence headquarters, and the army. She thinks she's learning to tell the difference between her people and theirs. It's something her mother can do like breathing; walk into a corner store in London and say thank you, uncle, in the right language; trace someone back to their parents' village within the first minute of conversation. It's easier here than London: the same features happen again and again. And in the north, the default features are her mother's, her uncles', her grandfather's. Here, in this glassier, shinier suburb, they are the features of the other people. The killing people. She stops looking at faces. It's a trap, recognition.

The afternoon brightens up again once they're in the suburbs of the capital. Janaka notices she's awake and resumes his pointing things out: villas in the Portuguese style and canals built by the Dutch. The boarding school is in an unusually Christian neighbourhood. They call it Little Rome. On every street corner are little shrines protected by plastic sheeting, fogged up in the heat like the Marys have been breathing.

Janaka doesn't need to announce the school; it proclaims itself, a sudden curve of white plaster, pillars, a high defensive wall.

'I'll meet you afterwards?' she suggests to Mia.

'I'll go and explore.'

Archan's new school has a reception area with air conditioning and a leather couch. The receptionist asks for Kolia's ID, and tells her in perfect English that Archan's teacher can send him down in a few minutes, when his lesson ends.

Kolia waits, shivering in her short sleeves. The place is staggeringly different from her grandmother's. The students are all in crisp white shirts, maroon ties. They're almost all brown kids, which distracts from the private international school atmosphere only slightly. She scrutinises each child that wanders past her, wondering which ones are Enzos. Good that the receptionist asked for her ID, she thinks. At Ammama's school you could probably grab them from the front gates.

She's started sizing the next child up for potential Enzo-ish warning signs (ringlets, smug gleam) for a good second before she realises it's Archan. He's in a cleaner, neater uniform than any he wore in England, coming down the stairs with another student. He grins at Kolia, then turns and smiles at the other boy, who takes his cue to leave.

'Hi, Kol!'

His face doesn't shine with belonging, the way Ammama's did. But perhaps he's caught a tan.

'Oh, sweetie,' says Kolia, speaking into the top of his head. 'I missed you. Are you okay?'

'Yes,' Archan says. 'Mum said I could call you when I got here but I haven't topped up my phone yet.'

'It's all right, you don't need to. I'm going to take you home. Like, tomorrow.'

He closes his mouth. He does look a bit different. It's just a tan and a smile maybe. And a sort of lowering of the shoulders.

'I'm on the ping-pong team. We're going on a trip next week for a competition.'

'Okay,' says Kolia. 'Well, we can't stay an extra week for a ping-pong competition.'

'If we get through to the next round, we go north as well. So I can see Ammama.'

'Come on, Archan. Don't you want to see the Baby?'

'Yes, but.' He struggles. 'I'll see him in a month anyway. In the summer holidays.'

Archan nods again, looking at the water. There are cranes on the closest strip of land, perched all over the beached fishing boats. Much further out, a thicket of trees towards the other side of the lake. Like a floating forest, almost too far to see.

'There are water monitor lizards over there,' he says, pointing to the forest. 'And monkeys.'

'Can the monkeys swim?'

'I don't know, but they get enough food from people on boat trips.' (He pulls up a thin handful of the grass.) 'Anyway.' (He shreds it over his shoes.) 'I think she's right. Not that it's my fault. But that I'm safer here. And I like it.'

'Okay.'

'The principal says he can get me a SIM card with data, so I can message you.'

'Okay.'

They sit and watch the shore on the other side of the chain-link fence. A stray dog noses between the peeling boats, looking for scraps. He wanders up to the water's edge. The lake laps the sand, washes over his paws; his hunted look disappears the second his feet are wet.

5.

'And then we played ping pong,' Kolia says. 'And he is really good.'

'Fuck me,' says Mia.

The bar is nearly empty, the atmosphere confused but in-offensive: a sports bar with flowers on the tables and dim lights behind coloured glass. Kolia and Mia are sitting at the counter. Their drinks have umbrellas in, which adds to Kolia's sense of this all having just been some bizarre, aborted holiday.

'The thing is, it makes so much sense that he'd want to stay. It seems obvious now; I don't know why I didn't think of it. He has everything that he doesn't get at home: structure, consist-ency, meals at the right times.' At the thought of his well-fed little face, the surprise of his clean uniform, Kolia can feel her heart hardening against her mother again. After all the love and guilt she'd felt at the temple, it's a relief.

'And maybe he likes being close to his roots.'

'Maybe. I hope he's not just been seduced by the ping-pong table. I told him I could get one for home.' She sighs. 'I can't believe I dragged you along for this.'

'I'm glad you did,' says Mia. 'It's good to see that Archan's found the right place.'

'Maybe. He'll be home in a month anyway, so he can change his mind if he needs to.'

'It doesn't seem strange to me at all that he would feel happier here. Or that he would be more suited to life here.' Mia pauses, chooses her words carefully, playing with a pink plastic stirrer. '*I* feel happier here. Especially when we were back north with your grandmother.'

Kolia takes a long sip.

'Like, it can't be a bad thing for Archan to grow up away from London. It's poisoning people for sure. It's such a mean, brittle place right now. Churning out pointless upswings, pointless downswings. Look at Gabriel's last thing. "Ten Totally Bizarre Pen Name Origin Stories". We're surviving on nonsense. It must be about to collapse.'

'Ye-es,' says Kolia slowly. She tips a slurry of sugar and crushed ice onto the back of her tongue.

'I feel like a person can matter more here. Or, can make a difference. I know I don't know anything, I know I haven't been here long, I know that maybe I only feel like this has been meaningful because, like, my environment is new, and because we've been working with actually sweet children, who could use our help, instead of prepping little demons for their entry into the literal cycle of privilege. But also that is enough for me, I think. Learning and helping.'

She's getting drunker and drunker, opening and shutting the umbrella like a flower, but Kolia believes the words that are coming out of her mouth because she's heard them before, in fits and starts, and delivered lightly, the way you deliver an opinion you hope someone will refute.

'Nothing I do in London has an effect. Every action is swallowed up. Like, I help this guy, I hurt this guy, I go to a party – these things might as well not happen. We're always gesturing towards purpose, but we never get there. That's why it's so easy to fall in love with a boy who's actually giving you nothing. He just has to make a little feint towards giving you a *bit* of something and it's like, *Oh, okay, this seems about as meaningful as anything else.*'

'I don't feel like I've been gesturing,' says Kolia, taking the umbrella out of Mia's hand. 'I'm treading water, mainly. And also, if you mean Gabriel, you can just say Gabriel.'

Mia laughs, eyes wild. 'I mean when people say: this is what I'm doing now. Like if someone says, I'm trying to be really productive. Or if someone says, I'm rejecting productivity, I'm embracing the bare minimum. Or if someone says, I really want to fall in love. It's just saying: this is what I think could be my purpose. But they're not purposes, they're just stretching out towards purpose.'

'You're being so mean.'

'Right! It's London, it's making me horrible.' Mia pauses, addresses the fake lilies. 'Theo's dad touched me up last week. Not – not anything crazy. He just pulled me into his lap. Well, he pulled me onto one knee and Theo onto the other, like having his kid there would cancel the whole thing out.' She stares into the vase. Pink cloth, plastic spikes. 'Anyway, it's not that; it's everything, everyone searching – Theo, thinking he could make his fortune from peacock feathers, and Gabe when he drinks. Mum, with her accent lighting. It's good that Archan's staying here. I think I want to stay here for a while as well.'

Kolia doesn't ask Mia what makes her think that people here are searching any less. She looks down at the pattern she's been making on the back of her hand with the pointy end of the cocktail umbrella, and then she presses her other hand gently into Mia's cheek.

'I'll go back with Janaka,' says Mia, taking the patterned hand and rubbing out the indents with her thumb until Kolia's skin is smooth again. 'Once he's picked up the textbooks.'

'Okay. Don't you need to come home first, though? To sort out visas and whatnot?

Mia shakes her head. 'I think I'm scared to go back home.'

And she makes the face Archan was making when he talked about leaving school, even though he'd be going back to neglect and disorder and Mia could just go back to Shoreditch.

Kolia doesn't press her. Everyone must feel this way at least a bit, though it unsettles her that Mia's feeling it here, in a country that's really Kolia's, but she doesn't say anything about that. There had been something ticking in the hollow of Mia's throat when she was talking about Theo's father touching her, something familiar, a great shuddering held breath, and Kolia knew when she had seen it before – she had seen it on that horrible afternoon with the sun-cream man. So she doesn't press her, only makes light jokes about Mia being a hippie and a sucker, about how she's been tricked into staying by the little girl that had hugged her at the end of the lesson. They both get more drinks. The flight isn't for hours. When they say goodbye, Kolia wraps her arms around Mia tightly, forgetting not to cling. She feels Mia push something into her hand and after they pull apart, she sees that it's the eye mask: satin and sequins for the trip home.

It's getting dark when she leaves the bar, the sky all dulling rose. The faces don't look like killing faces any more, just faces.

6.

Across the ocean, the Baby falls asleep watching TV on the colonial couch, face tipping forward into Sheba's fur. Lalita crawls through the dichondra room like a woman in the wreckage of a plane crash. Its windows open out onto night-time: the quiet road and all its hedges. She shuffles on her knees until the floorboards bite her, clutching at a T-shirt her son forgot to pack. She presses her mouth into the corner of his mattress.

PART 6: PARSLEY, SAGE, ROSEMARY AND THYME

1.

Things were strange for a while after Kolia landed. Leaving Archan and Mia behind had lent a graver edge to all the usual little comedowns that follow touchdown, the lights off in her empty flat, the bins that should have been emptied before she'd left. She catalogued the walls for anything that had changed in her absence – the darker-seeming patch of damp in her bedroom – and their bareness was suddenly appalling; every odd Blu-Tacked postcard a child's stab at homemaking.

And that overtired child was raising its voice again, its old fractiousness stirred by the image of Mia, shining, bestowing her knowledge on the grateful eight-year-olds against a backdrop of lakes and parrots. It was saying: she's at the lake with purpose and you're here with none. It was saying: she should have known that it wasn't her place to stay. She's doing what she always does, drifting around, collecting experiences – like Fillipo said.

No: Fillipo had been wrong, it was never like that; she was genuinely ingenuous, thought Kolia, remembering the sun-cream man again. Remembering his big red hand dripping, coming down over the back of Mia's neck. Then the running, the screaming, the panting walk home. They'd spent the whole of that night in Kolia's kitchen, neither able to sleep, telling each other everything that had ever happened to them as quickly as they could speak. She felt light, suddenly, at the idea that the girl she'd stayed up with in that kitchen had drifted at last into something that was right.

Putting the fractious child to bed helped her twice.

It hadn't suddenly made her flat less empty, of course. She could still smell the staleness of the aeroplane hold on her clothes; she couldn't look at her phone, which was filling up with texts from all the wrong people – question marks from Francesca, and photographs of Enzo's lopsided curls.

But then she did look, and there was the message that could only have been a karmic reward for letting Mia go gracefully, for not having said, 'No, that's my grandma.' An email from the foundation in Maastricht: a promise and a starting date, and more excitement than she'd ever imagined might be warranted by her mountboard Xeroxes.

It was perfect, perfect timing. It was like one of Ammama's stories: milk and honey, foxes and metaphysically guaranteed fairness. Kolia had held the phone to her heart and felt it beam. She'd turned on all the lights in the flat at last, and then started ordering everything she thought she might need: a new sketchbook, a portable door lock, bear spray; with every purchase, thinking of monasteries and Old Masters. Shared studio space and the basilica! She'd be leaving in a month.

She'd gone to Gabriel's flat to tell him the news. He had crémant in the fridge already; he poured them both big glasses and squeezed her hand sincerely as he sat down. Under the table, he hooked his foot round her ankle. He was so proud of her, he said.

'You know, I always forget that you went to art school. Those days were the best. You and Phillip were the artists, and me and Mia were the plus ones. The common folk.'

'She used to help me with my homework.'

'No way.' Gabriel laughed. He jumped back up, got a super-market chicken sandwich out of the fridge. 'You want some of this?'

'I'm good.'

'Me and Fillipo did a bit of that. You ever do that one where you're supposed to talk about something for ten minutes but you can't bring it back to yourself?'

'Yes! Houses.'

'We had yellow. But we did it so that you can only talk about it in relation to yourself. Turned it on its head, you know?'

Kolia watched Gabriel tear into the sandwich. She felt the same laughter rising in her that had once been reserved for roadkill art. Mia had been right. Kolia wished she was here.

'So like, yellow is the bike I used to ride across the Heath, buttercups, the chin trick. Yellow plate that my mum always serves birthday cake on, yellow spines on my grandmother's Country House classics, I suppose yellow pages too. *Kill Bill*, that's not super personal except that I always had such a crush on Uma Thurman. Less so in *Pulp Fiction* – what can I say, I like blondes. I guess blonde is a kind of yellow?'

The crémant fizzed in a single spine, like there was an aspirin at the bottom of her glass. Someone, possibly his mother, had put potted bougainvillea on Gabriel's windowsill, and now there was something Greek about the room. All the unfurnished bareness of his flat, transmuted into a kind of Ionian simplicity. Would it have been his mother? His mother, who made sculptures that rejected being held?

Kolia preferred her flat anyway, she realised, every Blu-Tacked poster. It didn't matter. She'd be in Maastricht soon. It was a perfect noun, Maastricht, a perfect word: just foreign enough to be totally free of association, no suggestive common etymology, no Amadora or Limerick or Montesilvano, only Old Dutch strangeness.

Some of the shredded chicken was escaping the sandwich. Gabriel pushed it back in with his fingers, then put his hand on her thigh. Kolia thought of the compulsions that guided the way she treated statues of her gods: touching them with washed hands, keeping them upright when she dusted, making sure no crumb ever shared their tray. Possibly Gabriel had some directly opposite compulsion.

She missed Mia acutely. It hit her with the same acuteness that she wouldn't miss Gabriel at all.

He told her that he wasn't looking for anything serious after they finished the crémant. Long distance wouldn't suit him, he said, and in any case, it didn't seem right to settle down with the state the world was in. Really, they both owed it to themselves to explore a variety of feelings and people and bodies, to fit a life's worth of romances into the next ten years. ('That's how long we've got,' he'd said, looking up at Kolia from between her legs. 'Ten years. I've been reading some René Guénon, and it's really interesting stuff.' His chin digging into her stomach.)

She suspects that if Gabriel did truly believe they had ten years left to live, he'd be wifing her up so that he could be sure of having someone to hold him in the final fiery hours of Armageddon, someone to hide him from the gas-rich meteorites. She suspects that his cosmic timelines talk is a mystical cover for an actually quite pragmatic accounting of the future: ten years of freedom before he begins to look for a partner to share in childcare and a mortgage. She's heard him use the word 'bachelorhood' unironically in the past. Kolia didn't break any plates. Her sketchbook was arriving that day. She'd removed his chin from her stomach, got dressed and left his house, smooth and practised as any child of divorce.

She isn't speaking to her mother either, incidentally.

2.

No one's happier about Maastricht than Kolia's dad. He's so pleased that he goes pink, hugs her as if he can physically confer his pride, and starts researching the Limburg public transport system. She can see that it's unloosed some knot of parental worry. They must do something to celebrate, he says, tugging at his eyebrows absently, still smiling.

They go to the lido, which holds outdoor concerts every summer. The weather's perfect when Kolia and her father get there, early evening, cool blue. They arrive in time to watch the last swimmers finish their laps, a handful of pale bodies gliding through the rising steam, all in their sixties. Kolia watches a particularly vigorous swimmer haul himself out and shake dry, water flying off his liver-spotted back in beads.

Halfway down the field, her father identifies the best place for their blanket. The average age doesn't drop off this side of the pool; the grass is invisible under a mass of camping chairs and Thermos flasks and white-haired heads.

'I bet I'm one of the youngest here,' says her father, pleased.

It would make sense; Dolorosa had all their biggest hits in the seventies. Kolia doesn't see anyone else who might be within ten years of twenty, though she's surely not the only person her age who grew up with their CDs in the car. Dolorosa's a folk-rock band; they'd played with Joni Mitchell, setting traditional ballads to electric guitar, so naturally she'd pictured the field outside the lido full of ageing hippies – braided beards, lots of silver jewellery. Instead, she's surrounded by unbroken normcore; retirees, with Thermoses of hot squash rather than shroom tea.

The band open with fast, seething fiddles and a song about a drowned sailor. It's an ode to all the dry land of England: corn-fields, green hills, meadows and mountains. Kolia watches the audience nod along and wishes they were the hippies she'd imagined, spinning in circles, twirling their vintage scarves. The sedate unison of this audience, tapping their wrinkled fingers steadily on the armrests of their camping chairs, is very *Wicker Man*; the cornfields ballad is beginning to feel faintly nationalist.

The week before seems like a dream. This evening is so removed from the speed and heat and shock of that other coun-try. There's something familiar and inevitable about tonight. The gathered listeners reek of ease, the field is still and placid beneath the wild fiddle strings. To be here, with her Phileas Fogg father, is to heed the part of Kolia that is the whitest brown person someone knows. It's not quite comfortable, but it's not uncomfortable either. Kolia's the only brown person, and also the youngest person, the most attractive. She's pleasantly exceptional. It had been an odd feeling, in the island country, to see parts of herself everywhere she went.

Dolorosa are moving through the songs of mythical England, which is a place she can still see more clearly than anywhere else. War, death, enchantment, betrayal, poverty. Her dad's driv-ing music – tales bound up with watching landscapes going by, green speed, even paint-strokes. 'Death and the Maiden', 'Tam Lyn', 'Matty Groves': these had been as real in Kolia's imagined childhood world as pennies from heaven and birds in the sycamore tree. They feel realer, even now, than the world from which she's just returned; Ammama's world, rubble and rambutans. The reality of that other country fades like a tan, leaving behind the disappointment of losing a brother and a friend to it.

Lalita had liked Dolorosa too, once. Kolia doubts she listens to them any more, but she had sung along back when it had been the three of them in the car, in her low bluesy way. Her favourite song had been 'The Outlandish Knight', Dolorosa's update of a Georgian ballad. It was godly work, she'd said, preserving and recording a dying tradition. It's a surprising take from a woman who thinks maypole dancing is racist, but it had to do with the island country, of course – the burning of the public library in the northern capital. Its archives had been some of the best in Asia, recording the history and the language of the country's minority population. There are long gaps now in their past. Kolia remembers her mother in the car, talking over the music, telling her that afterwards, when whole families were killed in the war, the records of them had already been burned to ashes and so there was no obstacle to their complete erasure. Oh, she doesn't want to think about her mother right now, or palm-leaf manuscripts on fire. She wants to go back to feeling pleasantly exceptional, her brownness an uncomplicated distinction. She takes out her phone to film the guy who's just got the bagpipes out and sees that Lalita is texting her.

She only has to read the first message to know what's happening. The tone's unmistakeable. The tip-offs are all there: the same red flags that had presaged the river, the bleach, the blister packs, the lying in the road. *I've always loved you. You'll be better off without me.*

On stage, Dolorosa are working themselves into a frenzy, a crescendo of Merrie England. The texts are arriving with increasing urgency. It's always the way with Lalita. She drives everyone away and then she misses them. The bagpipes are wailing. Kolia sees – the river, the bleach, the pills, the road. She mustn't forget that the pills had only ever been antihistamines, the road an empty cul-de-sac. The wailing crests and then ceases; Dolorosa start a new round. Kolia father taps his foot happily as John Barleycorn gets pitchforked through the heart. *You can tell the boys I've moved abroad*, her mother texts. *To Europe*. It's always this way. She mustn't forget that it's always this way, only ever an attempt at manipulation. Parasuicide, a suicidal gesture. Lalita never really gets hurt; Kolia does, every time. Kolia should honour the way her heart had hardened again by the end of the visit to her mother's country, seeing how distance had made Archan happy at last, seeing that he could have been happy all along. If she always comes running, the gesture will hold its value: Lalita will never stop making it. The newest text says *I know it would be better for everyone if I just disappeared*. Kolia shouldn't have to run. She shouldn't have to do complicated things. She could forget the texts, forget the other country, let herself be absorbed into this field of unvarying, placid, squash-drinking English whiteness.

Kolia turns her phone off, tunes back into the mandolin, and doesn't think about messages that can't deliver. She tries to submit to this, the blue evening, the steam on the water. Dolorosa sing of maidens gazing from castle windows, north winds. And of Death, waylaying travellers. Sailors, knights, husbands off to war. Death: a man made of cold red clay.

Gilded horns, friendless wanderers, lonely bowers.

Death, at the foot of a bed.

3.

Many years ago, in a department store that's now closed, Lalita had decided that the classic waterfall chandelier had unsound political associations. Her daughter had just disappeared into the soft-furnishing section; her husband was looking at his watch. Lalita had nearly given up hope when she spotted it, streamlined and modern, glittering mutedly. Hexagonal crystals, irregularly cut, suspended on invisible wires from a single bar of stainless steel. It was a light fitting from a classless society.

She hadn't been sure about the new house. Her husband loved the area and the schools were good but they were hours by train from anyone she knew, and she was wary of being beholden to her parents. But when she'd looked closely at the little glass prisms floating between her face and the store ceiling, the light had burned her eyes and she'd seen her future, seen how friends would come to their house and drink wine and smile at the books on the shelves, and her daughter would draw on the walls and she wouldn't scold her, she'd just paint over it, or even display it, and they'd keep the living room doors open to the garden so that the air was fresh and they could go out and stand on the grass, and there on the lawn her husband would catch her around her waist, and over it all would be the tinkling sound of the chandelier, a light fitting from the future.

*

In the future, the John Lewis chandelier hangs undisturbed in the living room at No. 25. It's an unusual shape. The room has been empty for days. Weeks? The crystals change colour and no one sees. In natural light, small flares glow in the bellies of each prism. When the sun flares in the garden, the lower crystals burst, dichroic, cast blue and white onto the carpet. There's no one in the living room to push their bare foot into the reflection or to feel how the carpet's warmer there. There's no one to turn the lights on in the evening, so the crystals hang in the dark, going quiet and heavy. They might tremble, minutely, on their strings. They might catch some faint line of moonlight and pass it on, a series of reflections, crystal to crystal to mirror. They might shift that faint light around until it lands on the big dull shards of a Perspex cube, which has broken and been left in pieces on the floor. They might; there's no one to see.

No. 25 stays empty. Days pass through the rooms, make their circuits of hallways, recede unobserved. Light eases over the floors, floods up the walls, withdraws, disappears; the thermostat and landline screens flicker uselessly. Tiny, spiny things continue to occupy the garden, unaffected by the absences, or made braver. Empty of its contradicting visitors (one woman who sees it as full of sun and one who sees it in permanent shadow), the garden's no longer some wild, emotionally fraught mirror-place. It's just: grass, thistles, brambles. The scrubby lawn shivers in a soft breeze. Light pools and dapples on the slant of the blue shed; behind the shed, dark collects in the small bifurcations of the blackberry stems.

The garden, the patio, the passage that runs along the side of the house up to the road – these outside places are themselves. They don't carry the knowledge of absence or emptiness, the way it's carried by an empty chair, or a broken ornament, or the chandelier with no one to turn it on. The foliage of the front hedge has lost its shape, but the hedge's core, its interior structure, is the same as ever. A rough, twisted grid of branchlets, cracked dead bark; small pathways of younger stems, curling offshoots, bracts with serrated edges. That day she'd run away from home and not made it past the front garden, Kolia had hid under the hedge on her side of the garden wall. And she'd looked so closely at the hedge, not the leafy part, but the impenetrable geometry at eye level – the underside, the supportive mesh of twigs and forking stems – that she'd felt she could draw it from memory. It looks the same now, twenty years later; passers-by appear through small gaps in the greenery as brief flashes of colour. No one walking down the street would know that No. 25 is empty. The bins in the front garden are half full; the rubbish is going bad, but not yet smelling. The curtains in the front room are not drawn but the hedge obscures any view into the house from the street.

At the side of the front room, a medicine cabinet stands out of the light. The wood is heavy and old, like a lot of No. 25. In the many compartments of the medicine cabinet, small things are singing, trinkets and postcards. It's the song of flotsam, of nobody having looked at them in years. It sounds like potential and nostalgia and the same guilt that comes from leaving a Tupperware box in the back of the fridge for so long that it can never be opened again. The Ziploc of brass screws, the hotel sewing kit, the baby tooth in its miniature envelope: all sing, louder without anyone to hear them. The sound echoes in the empty room, floats on motes of dust.

Underneath is another thin, high humming, not from inside the medicine cabinet but from behind it. This is the same song with more ghosts in it: discordant horror-film notes, the kind of music that plays low over the shot of the door that doesn't open. The song's coming from the lipstick message, of course: the oath or curse or plea scrawled across the wall behind the cabinet. Even now, smudged over time, faded by sunlight, the texture suggests that the lipstick was expensive. No one's read it for years. At the back of her mind, Kolia knows it has something to do with leaving.

A low desk has been dragged into the middle of the room and left there at an angle. Heavy and old like the medicine cabinet and done up in great streaks of paint, which are more careful and less beautiful than the hidden lipstick. Archan had been sent away before he'd revised his work, so the oil bird and cherry blossom are still patchy smears, and the backdrop's only sweeps and smudges that don't reach all the corners. The drawers are empty except for a few old matchboxes, marked with odd crests, logos of long-shut hotels in Algarve, Jaffna, Freetown. The matches inside are mostly too damp to light.

There's a sense of damp throughout the whole house. Warm, windless damp, like sea air. No. 25 is miles from the sea but the sand is back in the corners of the front room. The wallpaper in the corridor looks like it might come loose and the silt of broken seashells has crept back up into the kitchen sink. Calcite and nacre glinting at the plughole.

The brass gods in the kitchen have gone pearly too, from dust and twilight. They guard the microwave and a wicker basket of medication, significantly depleted. Two of the statues had come with Ammama from the country of Lalita's birth: the destroying god, dancing with one foot on a demon, and his son, who removes all obstacles. Lalita had picked up the goddess of knowledge from a corner shop in Tooting, just in time for her daughter's GCSEs, and she'd bought the goddess of time, doomsday and death from a market in Harrow, on some ordinary day in the early 2000s when she'd felt she needed strength. The fifth had come from a tourist stall outside a temple in Malaysia. Lalita had never heard of the self-decapitating goddess before that trip. The statue on top of the microwave is nude with a necklace of skulls and her own head in her hand. Two brass spouts extrude from her open neck and into the mouths of her thumb-sized attendants, poorly welded to the statue's base. 'She's feeding them with her own blood,' the man at the market had explained. 'She's the goddess of self-sacrifice.' Lalita had nodded feelingly and handed over her ringgits. She hadn't seen her daughter in almost a year. She understood self-sacrifice.

Upstairs, the gods in the master bedroom have weathered abandonment better. Of course, they're used to it, shrined in a room that's locked up for most of the year, and perhaps it helps that they're paintings rather than statues: brighter colours, fewer surfaces to collect dust. But it's also true that the recent transformation of their realm suits them. The gods and gurus have been looking well ever since Lalita had broken the door of this room wide open, some time before the house fell empty. She'd busted the lock, splintered the wood; the big dark desk had been dragged downstairs. She must have spent hours in there afterwards, sweeping books off the shelves, clothes off the rails, laying waste, because the room's frozen in chaos. Like Cornelia Parker's exploded house, or like returning from holiday to a robbed, empty home. Even the bed has been ransacked, the sheets rucked up, the mattress half off the frame. Time's slow in the abandoned house, but Ammama's smashed-up room is a shrine to frenzy. The days (weeks?) – the silent shifts in light – leach over a mad, disordered still. All the pillaging has shattered its former microclimate: that odd, warm sea-wind rushes in through the open door, nearly off its hinges, and in this dry and airless space it's almost refreshing. The gods look happy. The silverfish have fled.

Down the corridor, the air is stiller. It swells the wood on the banister.

There's no clue in Lalita's room as to why the house is empty. It's a totally ordinary bedroom. The bed is a low, nearly legless Japanese frame, upholstered in white leather, now tea-stained. There are wind chimes, a framed butterfly, a Mexican print with some Socialist slogan in green letters. There's a pile of underwear and dirty socks. There are too many shoes, mostly years old. There are photographs of all her children.

There's nothing uncanny here, no ghost in the mirror, no mysterious coastal detritus. Just a woman's empty bedroom, quiet with what's happened to her.

4.

Ravi misses his dog.

His dad had been all set to send Sheba to a short-stay kennel but Ravi had argued and cried until finally he'd worn him down, and they'd found a neighbour who was able to look after Sheba for a while. The next two weeks, at least. Maybe more. That's one of the things annoying Ravi today: nobody knows how long anything's supposed to take.

For example, he's been waiting to see this lady for half an hour now. Ravi watches the clock, folding up leaflets into concertinas with his little square hands. The town hall is a brown-brick building five minutes from the swimming pool. He's walked past it a hundred times without realising. A town hall should be grander, he thinks. You should be able to tell what it is.

'One day you'll come here to get your driving licence,' his dad had said, the first time he'd dropped him off. He patted Ravi awkwardly on the shoulder and said he'd pick him up when he was done. Ravi's been in and out a few times since, always waiting at least twenty minutes. His caseworker beams ecstatically when she finally calls his name, as if to make up for the wait. She tries too hard, the caseworker; Ravi sees it. He smiles back to make her feel better.

Ravi wants everyone to feel better. He smiles a lot. His dad thinks it's because he's too young to understand what's going on but Ravi's smart for his age. That's why he doesn't say that he misses his brother or that he wishes he didn't have to do all these meetings by himself – because Ravi knows that then they'd make Archan come back, and he thinks Archan's probably happier wherever he is. He pictures Archan going to school on the beach, which quickly becomes Archan going to school in the sea, and then under the sea. The desks are made of coral and grow out of the seabed but no one can figure out how to stop all the worksheets floating up to the surface so Archan never gets any homework.

The room where Ravi has his meetings with the caseworker is kind of like the school counsellor's office, except the school counsellor doesn't act like she thinks your mum is shit. To be fair, Ravi's not sure how much the school counsellor knows about what's happened, only that his dad had asked her to see him twice a week since he'd left No. 25. He's not a hundred per cent sure how much about *he* knows what's happened.

Ravi had been at a birthday party. Conrad's parents didn't seem sure about letting him leave alone, but it wasn't far from No. 25 and Mum wasn't answering the phone, so Ravi pretended that she was parking at the other end of the street.

'But she's not very good at parking, so she can't come in – I have to just go and get straight in the car – she's waiting to pick me up I think – thank you for the cookie cake,' he said, and he smiled so that Conrad's parents would feel better.

When Ravi got home, all the lights in the house were off. He could hear Sheba whining at the end of the hall. He followed the noise to the living room without stopping to take off his shoes. Mum was in the nursing chair. Her eyes were closed. Something felt wrong, but he called out to her and made himself sound loud and cheerful. Less cheerful the second time.

He twisted the plastic handles on his party bag, frowning at the body in the chair, and then he put his hands on her shoulders and shook her. It felt very bad to shake his mother, who didn't even like hugging much. If she'd been awake she would have shoved him off. The fourth time he shook her she stirred a bit, and her eyes moved underneath her eyelids.

He sat down on their new couch to call the ambulance, feet high off the floor, swinging while he answered questions about breathing and was there any blood? He had to go back up to his mother to check her breathing: it was warm against his hand, weak but with its usual smell of coffee and sleep.

She was slightly more responsive by the time the paramedics came. Ravi nearly wished that she wasn't, that she was as scarily still as she'd been when he'd found her, so that the ambulance people could see how bad it had been. He tried to be especially helpful in case they thought he was overreacting, putting Sheba in the front room out of the way and offering to make coffee, though none of the medics wanted any. They wore dark green vests and spoke in code; she lurched when they moved her, and said something about Chinese food. At some point she'd started shivering very hard, still mostly unconscious. Her pulse wasn't good, apparently. Ravi packed her a night-bag with clean clothes and her inhalers. One of the paramedics cooed, which he thought was unprofessional, but he didn't say anything.

They put Ravi's mum in a wheelchair to load her into the ambulance; the paramedic who had cooed said that she'd wait with him until his dad arrived. The wheelchair jostled over the doorstep and Mum spoke without waking up. 'I'm a lawyer,' she was saying, almost indecipherably, eyes closed. There was a small trail of spit down her chin. 'I'm a lawyer,' she kept saying, as they took her away.

*

'Mummy had a bad reaction to some medicine,' Dad explained in the car.

'Vyvanse,' Ravi said helpfully. He'd memorised the word Vyvanse when he saw it in the medicine box; it was a good character name, for a paladin or a mage or something.

'No,' Dad had said. 'But the Vyvanse made her so excited that she took the other medicine.'

Ravi puts it together later that the Vyvanse had created the perfect storm. Just like a mage, working and powerful under her skin.

His dad's having a hard time looking after Ravi; he doesn't hide it well. His flat's too small for two people anyway, and Ravi doesn't want to get used to it – unfamiliar shower products and the wrong milk in the fridge. The deputy head from his school comes by, which is weird, like seeing a dog talk. ('Would you like some coffee?' Ravi asks her, hopefully.) She tells his dad that there are safe, reliable options for taking Ravi off his hands. He says he'll think about it.

Mum's in hospital. They can't visit her yet. Phones ring with incomprehensible news. She's in the Lilac ward. She moves to the Dolphin ward, which means she's getting better. It's never his mother's voice at the end of the line. Ravi imagines her there, like he has all the other times she's been to hospital. He's getting good at it. He thinks he can nearly remember being born.

After a while, they move back into No. 25. It makes sense: all Ravi's stuff is there, and Dad's flat isn't right for kids. It's also intensely weird. Even with both of them there, the house feels abandoned. The rooms are quiet with a strange, dull, silver-blue light that wasn't there before, and Ammama's room is finally open, but also carnage. Ravi secretly thinks that if he steps through that busted door he'll never come back out.

The social services meetings have slowed down. In their place are triweekly appointments with Child and Adolescent Mental Health Services. Ravi's glad Archan doesn't have to come to these, because he'd hate them. Archan doesn't know anything about what's happening. There's no point in telling him until he's back for the summer holiday. The CAMHS meetings are almost identical to the ones with the caseworker, talking over the same material in the same winding, endless loops, only in a concrete hospital wing instead of the town hall. The work of arranging them is almost worse. Somehow, Ravi's responsible for organising the CAMHS appointments, the town-hall appointments, his online self-assessments, the school counsellor's pointless check-ins. No one seems to notice they're sending these to a school email address. His father never asks how all these consultations are being scheduled, just drops him off and picks him up, and sits in his car swiping through dating apps in between. All of Ravi's tasks accumulate, overwhelm, but even as the mass of work increases, the texture remains crawlingly slow. Twenty minutes of hanging around before each appointment, a fly buzzing over the wall tile, the long white lace of emails, air conditioner in the waiting rooms on too strong. Nothing new said, nothing accomplished. No word from Mum.

It's different at school. Everyone's super excited when Ravi tells them what's happened. Your life is literally like a film, someone says. Ravi plays it cool.

'Mrs Dixon came to my house.' He laughs. 'Fucking lame.'

One day he says that he doesn't want to go to school, just to see what will happen.

His dad looks frustrated, presses Ravi's uniform into his arms, ignoring the mud on the back. (Dad says he can't figure out Mum's washing machine.) Eventually, Ravi grumbles and submits. He's doesn't want to cause trouble.

Usually Ravi likes the walk to school. It's the best time to think. Your body is on automatic, which frees up all the space in your head. He likes to make up scenarios where he's a hero, or a very cool villain. Sometimes he's saving everyone in the assembly hall from a school shooter; sometimes he's infiltrating the Red Dragon Syndicate. Sometimes he pretends he's a scavenger child, a mysterious orphan who survives on his wits and off the bounty of nature. The road to school suits that storyline perfectly because it's lined with these tall, fantastical hedges. Ravi bobs down the pavement next to them, slow enough to appraise each one for its treasure. There are all kinds of things you can make from hedges. Poison, itching powder, tea, perfume. The possibilities are electrifying. Ravi imagines – and, sometimes, believes – that he could kill a whole mafia with the holly berries from the bush outside the green house, or feed himself and Archan for weeks on rosehips if they ever ran away. One day, he'd found a necklace with a small circle pendant on their street, right at the edge of the kerb. When he gave it to his mother, that scavenged silver charm (possibly enchanted), he'd felt his imaginary world break its banks. He was a trader at a goblin market, a finder of lost things. It's strange being in his mum's house without her, but it's good to be on his road, with its long, flashing hedges. Even in their garden, Ravi's finding eye has been engaged. The other day he discovered a whole multi-tude of blackberries in the damp space behind their little blue shed. Thousands, maybe millions of blackberries. Maybe enough to sell, so they can make hundreds of pounds and buy anything they want, maybe delicious enough to make them famous, certainly enough for jams and sweets and tarts and cakes, but not jelly, because he doesn't like jelly. He's going to show the blackberries to Conrad tomorrow, and to his mother as soon as she's well.

5.

Kolia follows the painted footprints to the Dolphin ward. They're blue, of course, for dolphins. When she'd started out from reception there had been green and orange and purple footprints too, but they'd gone their separate ways, one after another, maternity and ophthalmology and oncology, and now she's suddenly alone. The overhead lighting is starkly, dizzyingly bright. Everything looks slightly unreal. The cellophaned flowers are sweating in her hand.

Lalita loves going into hospital, Kolia thinks. She loves to be looked after. She loves to have something wrong enough with her that she can be the victim, the baby, the darling of the ward. She loves being fed and measured and investigated; she loves the nurse electronically adjusting the trolley-bed so that she can be more comfortable. Lalita's real mother might forget that she exists, but in hospital they check ten times a day to see if she's okay.

A much younger Kolia, stared down by nasogastric and urinary catheters, had burst into tears once, thinking of what her mother had to endure. 'Don't worry,' Lalita had said, and taken her into both arms. 'Hospitals aren't so bad. They always make me think of having ice cream after I got my tonsils out. I even really like the food.'

She doesn't want me to be scared, Kolia had thought at the time, and loved her mother. But after the seventh or eighth time that Lalita plumped for an extra night in a hospital bed, Kolia realised she'd been telling the truth. She didn't mind it there at all. Lalita found reasons to self-admit all the time, long before she'd learned the trick of suiciding, and so Kolia had been extensively parented from the inside of one hospital or another. In the bathroom of a rehab facility, the responsibility of being separated from her daughter for another two months dawned on Lalita very suddenly. This is what a period looks like, she told Kolia, sounding more like a sixth former instructing a first-year than a mother, and dropping her underwear to demonstrate. (The dark stain didn't look anything like blood.) Over a tray lunch in a respiratory ward, she told Kolia how to check the Baby's hair for nits. And because she liked it there, she didn't notice that for every hospitalisation her daughter cried, panicked, couldn't sleep.

Dolphin Ward is silent and shadowy in a way that Kolia prefers to the hospital corridor. The lights are off, though it's midday; the high, small windows are covered, but some daylight creeps milkily through the blinds. Gloom, grey and dreamlike, cut with bedrot. There are six beds, each hidden behind its own individual curtain. A nurse gestures to one of them.

Kolia's not sure if this is the ward that she'd visited before. She guesses not. This time was different from the others, after all. *The big strip tease*, she thinks, approaching the curtain; *the theatrical comeback in broad day*. She draws it back on its railing.

Lalita's lying on her side, her face hidden in her arm. She looks like she normally does in hospital beds; frail and small, and washed out by the pale surgical gown. You can't tell from this angle that there was anything different about this time. Except that Kolia's face is suddenly wet.

Kolia puts the flowers down on the bedside table. The horrid air rushes up at her, that unsettling mix of sterility and infection, and everything frilled and toothless – the limp violets, the surgical masks. She falls down onto her mother's bed.

From behind one of the other curtains, the sound of a woman crying. Kolia puts out her hand, touches Lalita's back.

'Amma?' says Lalita. She doesn't turn around.

'No, it's me.'

'Kolia.' She sighs the name. She doesn't attempt to identity her further, just submits to having her back stroked.

'Will you . . . Can you sit up?'

Lalita breathes out, or maybe nods – some shudder, anyway, into the crook of her arm – and then she heaves herself straight, not upright, but her face is unsheathed now, and she's looking at Kolia. For a moment, Kolia braces herself for the feedback that always occupies the first minute of her mother laying eyes on her ('You have such dark circles, sweetheart') and then she remembers, or understands, that in fact that feedback will never come again, because her mother will never be able to see her face again, because her mother is blind.

Absolutely silently, Kolia starts to cry.

'Do you have my clothes, darling?'

Kolia hands them over wordlessly.

'I'll change now – do you want to pull the . . . ?'

It seems an effort for Lalita to take off the gown; she closes her eyes, as though to help her see. Kolia doesn't look away. Her mother's skin has the texture of a strange planet. An apron of slack skin hangs over her thighs, the record of three Caesareans; stretchmarks as wide as fingers cross the pouching sides of her stomach. There's a band of indentations left by her sports bra. Underneath, five inches of deep, fresh scar, barely a month old. She'd been telling the truth about the gallstones, then. They'd had to do open surgery instead of keyhole, apparently, because of all the C-section scar tissue. Before Lalita's body disappears into the big T-shirt, Kolia remembers – abruptly, violently – lying on her mother's stomach in the bathtub. It's a memory of her mother, not the person, but the warm, breathing topography of her. For a kid, a mother's body begins as terrain. By the time perspective develops and it's the body of a whole person, their separateness is shocking, their sudden fallibility. Kolia looks at Lalita's belly, now covered in soft cotton, and remembers first noticing the bulge of it, the flabby overhang of past childbirths, remembers the secret, creeping distaste she'd felt.

If she'd been slimmer, she'd be dead.

That's what the doctor told Kolia about the attempt. She'd taken diazepam this time, an amount that should have killed her. There was no questioning intention. There was no suggestion of 'gesture'. She had wanted to die, and she had texted Kolia that, and Kolia had stayed sitting in a folding chair and listening to folk music with her father.

If her mother had been slimmer, she'd be dead, but instead, she's blind.

'Don't cry.' Lalita wipes Kolia's face carefully. The peeling remnants of dark polish on her fingernails. She pauses, hand on her cheek, and then she says, 'Darling, your skin's very dry.'

Kolia crumples a little then, at the absolute unmistakeable ordinariness of her mother's fault-finding. She wants to ask her how it feels. She wants to ask if she meant to do it this time. She wants to ask what it means for the boys, who'll tell them, what paperwork she's been given for guidance on parenting blind. It was a problem of the ocular muscles, the doctor had said, not unheard of in patients recovering from benzodiazepine overdoses. Kolia's imagined every way that a 'problem with the ocular muscles' might appear and she wants to tell Lalita that she looks fine, beautiful, the most beautiful woman in the world.

She asks if Lalita wants her toothbrush.

Lalita doesn't hear her. The woman in the corner is out of breath now, heaving big, ragged sobs, and Lalita's listening to the crying, eyes closed, face tilted towards the sound like it's the sun. Kolia knows what will happen next. She watches her mother slowly, painfully, ease herself down from the bed.

'Will you help me over there?' Lalita says, facing Kolia at last. In her eyes, open and unseeing, the same thing as always: the Passion.

6.

The dark is heavier than she could have imagined, threateningly heavy, getting heavier. There's a tremendous pressure building in her eyes. It's impossible to tell if her eyelids are open or closed, but there's something like glue in the sockets, something like steel wool. She's blind and someone's sitting on her chest; blind and someone's pressing on her throat—

They lean back on their heels, lessen the weight. The room comes into focus slowly. At first, only as shapes of different opacities. Then as a wardrobe, a table. Some cruel tricks in between. A minute of paralysing fear before she understands that the broken, floating skull is just a fold in the hood of a coat on a hanger. The tunnel is just a fireplace, with an Art Deco iron surround.

The enjoyment that Kolia used to derive from her own short-sightedness, forgoing her glasses for a soft-focus world, is now totally foreign to her.

She'd moved her things back into No. 25 the week before. The master bedroom is a work in progress, the door still off its hinges, so she's set up in her old room, her room from the first time round. It feels as strange to her as space: every morning, bewildering.

A few nights after she'd moved in, she heard something – a sound coming from inside her room, though faint, as if it were far away or badly recorded. She went still under the duvet, listening, wondering if she should shout for help, but as the sound became clearer, there was something familiar in it: a thin voice, rising and falling, in conversation with a silent partner.

It was Kolia's voice.

She was hearing herself, herself as a child; the self that had lived in this room. Talking, singing, reading aloud to ward off the shadows of the neighbour's palm spikes. In Stone Tape theory, a ghost is just a recording a place makes. Time, xeroxed and detained.

The phantom voice seems excessive when Kolia's already here, already spectral. That feeling she used to get waking up in a strange bed, after a night out? That she'd gone back in time? It had come true. She'd had to turn down Maastricht, of course. There would be no art school, no shared studio, no basilica. There was only what there had always been: this house, and looking after her mother.

Lalita's blindness isn't darkness, exactly, though she gets black spots. It's convergence insufficiency, meaning that her eyes don't work together. Her vision is blurred, double, strained. She sees better in her periphery, twisting her head at alarming angles during conversation, although even this is too dizzying to sustain for more than a minute.

The doctor on Dolphin Ward had explained that it was possible, even likely, that Lalita would regain some vision over time; all being well, she could go from legally blind to partially sighted in less than a year. It wouldn't change much. Kolia knows she will never leave No. 25 now. Her life's work is staring her in the face with sightless eyes.

A crashing from below – the sound of breaking glass.

Kolia hurries downstairs. Dahlias and splintered crystal in the living room. Lalita's knocked down a vase of flowers on her way from the couch to the nursing chair. That's where she's sleeping, on the colonial couch; she'll live on the ground floor for the time being, until she's practised navigating the stairs.

'Keep your feet up,' says Kolia. 'I'll sweep.'

'I think it was the flowers,' Lalita says, curling her legs up like a child. 'Are they pretty?'

Kolia looks at the dahlias strewn across the carpet. They'd been a get-well gift from a solicitor. The red flowerheads bulge, sopping and scattered.

'Yes,' she says. 'They're pretty.'

'He has good taste, Patrick. Darling, do you think I could have breakfast now? And a coffee, please.'

(Waiting for the kettle to boil, Kolia imagines her mother smashing the vase on purpose, set on summoning up her porridge.)

For the rest of the morning, she helps Lalita draft her skeleton argument. All of Lalita's devices are now rigged with voice-to-text software, and there's a specialist coming tomorrow who'll introduce them to more technology designed to assist the blind. But there are PDFs and doctors' handwriting that can't be converted. There are photocopies of photographs of scars in black and white that image description generators will not understand. And so Kolia will never not need to be on hand. She reads the grounds for appeal aloud, thinking *scuts, vuks, tox, carx*.

Her mother makes a fantastic martyr. She rocks in the nursing chair, peering into the corners of the room without seeing them, changing direction before her gaze can harden into pain. She doesn't seem to understand everything Kolia says. Sometimes she twitches at sounds no one else can hear, and the way she winds her fingers in Sheba's fur makes Kolia think of a man she'd once seen tweaking in Hyde Park: blinking against the hallucinations, holding on tightly to fistfuls of grass. Mostly, though, she looks unnervingly happy. It must be her talent for delusion, or perhaps a result of her work, which has always inured Lalita to awful things, or at least allowed her to move on from them – to talk about rape by soda bottle one moment and sing Cole Porter the next. Now, as in Sicily, Kolia wishes that her mother would take things less in stride: that she would accept that some things are actually ruinously terrible, that there are times when it isn't appropriate to sing jazz, or ask if the flowers are pretty.

But Lalita just smiles: the Baby's in the garden, the dog's in the dog-bed, her daughter's returned. The satellites have returned, mostly, to their places. Kolia's helping with her newest case, a Tamil woman settled in Sicily, the mother of a client she'd had years and years before.

'Do you remember, Kolia,' she interrupts, 'that boy with the cigarettes?' Even as she talks, even as she looks around the room and cannot see it, No. 25 breathes and settles around her. 'That was a long time ago.' She laughs. She can laugh now, the house on her back, cradle, snail-shell. She likes the hospital but it's lovely to be at home.

'Don't strain your eyes,' Kolia says.

Lalita looks unphased. 'You know, it's really a godsend in terms of the practice. The Bar Standards Board aren't going to try me if I'm legally blind.'

Kolia looks at the gods doubtfully. The whole metal platter of them had been brought in from the kitchen like a tray lunch, resituated in the living room so that they could watch over Lalita as she slept. Shortly after they'd come home from the hospital, unable to understand why Lalita wasn't more upset, Kolia had asked her mother directly about her blindness for the first and only time.

'God will take care of everything,' Lalita had said.

God hadn't stopped her from going blind, thought Kolia, but okay. She's taking it on the chin. Like a saint would. (Of course, Kolia hadn't been there when Lalita woke up for the first time, when she'd realised she couldn't see. Though the nurse said she'd screamed and screamed.)

Kolia's less suited to her role as martyr's servant. Martyr's martyr. Mia had once read her a story that identified Judas as the overlooked hero of the redemption, since, by carrying out his pre-ordained task, which is to betray his saviour, Judas renounces peace, honour, heaven, while simultaneously setting into play the sequence of events which will be humanity's salvation. His sacrifice is even greater than Jesus's: facilitating rather than symbolic; the sacrifice that does not invite wonder, and which no one calls a miracle. Well, here's Kolia's thankless, ugly work, enabling a showy saviour. Mia had said that they were lucky if they could do anything that felt like purpose. But then, Mia's purpose had shown up as a cute kid hugging her around the waist, happy to be taught the alphabet.

Lalita falls asleep in the chair. On the couch, Kolia grits her teeth; her skull seems to contract until the printout in front of her blurs. She turns it over, begins drawing on the back, the pen landing so hard on the page that there are tacky black blotches at the beginning of each upstroke. No pre-emptory sketches, or points for proportion reference. There's no Maastricht, no one to see this. No reason now to correct mistakes. First thought, best thought; or rather, no thought, only hand and paper. Every line makes a sound like a scratch, or a door being pushed, and it starts to come back to her – yes, she had always loved to draw fingers that way, oyster knives falling off a hand – and these shapes, like the tendrilled cherub's breath that represents wind on old maps. The ink path crosses and recrosses itself, her jaw unlocking automatically; she's in the drawing completely, she's not sure how long, until she hears the nursing chair rock forward.

Lalita's awake, looking at her. But no, she can't see anything, of course; her eyes wash over the room, flicker, helpless.

'What are you doing?'

There's a slight fear in the question, an absolute unknowing, that hurts Kolia to hear.

'Come here,' she says, and Lalita crosses the room, feels for the wall, the side of the couch, until she's touching Kolia, very lightly. Kolia takes her mother's hand from her shoulder and puts it to the paper in front of her, fingertips first. She feels out the lines. It's true that there's no one to see what Kolia's made: it's a communication between the two of them, something that can only be passed from the daughter's pen to the mother's fingers. What could anyone else take away from the drawing? Only that it's imperfect, unrepeating, deeply grooved, deeply felt, overflowing the boundaries of the paper, unframeable.

'Fantastic,' Lalita says softly. 'Genius.'

Letting go of her mother's wrist, Kolia closes her eyes. The darkness isn't threatening or disorientating any more. There's no pressure or fear behind her eyelids, just warm, wide fatigue. She feels like she could go to sleep.

When she opens them again, she sees the Baby through the garden doors. He looks small and far away, a smudge by the broken-down shed; he's playing in the thistle.

'One second,' Kolia tells her mother. 'I'll be back in one second.'

She steps into the garden, inhaling earth and dew and dying pampas.

*

My mother sits without seeing. She is waiting for me to help her.

I'll be back in one second, I've said.

I will help her. I will help her without losing my sight.

If I wake up in the dark, I'm not going to lean into it! I haven't inherited anything that I can't hand back! I'm not Saint Judas, king of sacrifice, I'm not my mother, I'm not my mother's mother – and the Baby doesn't have to be me, hunched over by the hedges with an invisible and self-generated source of love.

I've rested my eyes now! I'm out in the garden now! I scoop Ravi up, dab at the juice on his chin; this is my purpose too, of course. Do I want to see the blackberries? More than anything I want to see the blackberries.

Acknowledgements

Many thanks to Hannah Chukwu – both for your kind and lovely first response to the novel back when it was *Care*, and for the unerring feedback that initiated its final form. I'm so grateful to have had you as an editor once more! Thanks also to my agent, Matthew Marland, for vital feedback on that first draft in Gordes. Thank you to David Bamford, for your attentiveness and precision, and thanks to Eleanor Gaffney for organising the final edit.

All my love and thanks to my mother. I don't say either enough.

Bringing a book from manuscript to what you are reading is a team effort.

Dialogue Books would like to thank everyone who helped to publish *Suckerfish* in the UK.

Editorial
Hannah Chukwu
Adriano Noble
Eleanor Gaffney

Contracts
Stephanie Evans
Sasha Duszynska Lewis
Isabel Camara

Sales
Megan Schaffer
Kyla Dean
Dominic Smith
Sinead White
Georgina Cutler-Ross
Kerri Hood
Jess Harvey
Natasha Weninger-Kong

Rights
Rebecca Folland
Helena Doree
Louise Henderson-Clark
Alexis Alderton

Design
Lucy Scholes
Sara Mahon
Sasha Egonu

Production
Kelly Llewellyn

Publicity
Charlotte Tonks

Marketing
Marcela Torres

Operations
Jairiza Rivera

Inventory
Victoria Stephenson
Dan Jones

Finance
Chris Vale
Jonathan Gant

Copy-Editor
David Bamford

Proofreader
Saxon Bullock

RAISING READERS
Books Build Bright Futures

Dear Reader,

We'd love your attention for one more page to tell you about the crisis in children's reading, and what we can all do.

Studies have shown that reading for fun is the **single biggest predictor of a child's future life chances** – more than family circumstance, parents' educational background or income. It improves academic results, mental health, wealth, communication skills, ambition and happiness.[1]

The number of children reading for fun is in rapid decline. Young people have a lot of competition for their time. In 2024, 1 in 10 children and young people in the UK aged 5 to 18 did not own a single book at home.[2]

Hachette works extensively with schools, libraries and literacy charities, but here are some ways we can all raise more readers:

- Reading to children for just 10 minutes a day makes a difference
- Don't give up if children aren't regular readers – there will be books for them!
- Visit bookshops and libraries to get recommendations
- Encourage them to listen to audiobooks
- Support school libraries
- Give books as gifts

There's a lot more information about how to encourage children to read on our website: **www.RaisingReaders.co.uk**

Thank you for reading.

---

[1] OECD, '21st-Century Readers: Developing Literacy Skills in a Digital World', 2021, https://www.oecd.org/en/publications/21st-century-readers_a83d84cb-en.html

[2] National Literacy Trust, 'Book Ownership in 2024', November 2024, https://literacytrust.org.uk/research-services/research-reports/book-ownership-in-2024